A Fraudulent Betrothal

A Fraudulent Betrothal

Natasha Andersen

ROBERT HALE · LONDON

ISBN 978-0-7090-8763-2

Robert Hale Limited
Clerkenwell House
Clerkenwell Green
London EC1R 0HT

www.halebooks.com

Typeset in 11/16pt Palatino
Printed and bound in Great Britain by
the MPG Books Group.

To Anna
For her support and encouragement

CHAPTER ONE

Twins

Constance stood silently by the window, gazing out on to the rose garden in still repose while the lazy haze of late afternoon light filtered through the hot sunshine of yet another brilliant summer day. Her wide, blue eyes, no longer so sure in their sight as in her youth, narrowed to follow the path of the two remarkably handsome young women trailing back to the house after a sunny afternoon spent working in the grounds. She sighed quietly to herself; Clarissa and Marianne had been left in her charge since babies, but, all too soon now, they would have to leave her for a wider world. She glanced with rheumy eyes towards the letter she still held in her hand and sighed again. She'd had her nieces to herself for twenty years; more time than she could ever have hoped for considering their beauty and talents, talents she herself had taken a hand in nurturing. But now they were both of them full grown women, ready to fly the nest.

One of the pair waved gaily towards her and she raised her hand in return, smiling at the self-evident difference in the twins, who, to all other intents and purposes, couldn't be told apart by anyone who didn't know them as well as Constance.

As a point of fact, as she well knew, even she could be fooled if they desired it. Constance recalled all the times they'd tricked her and smiled, all of a sudden appearing far younger than her matronly apparel suggested.

As she watched them the soft light of the evening sun seemed to add its own lustre to guinea-gold locks surmounting a pair of identical, even-featured, flawlessly skinned faces, each with a gloriously sunny smile in place as they continued to exchange their bantering asides. Constance was still too far off to spot the colour of their eyes, but she knew they were green; vivid, sparkling orbs that held thrall over most of the eligible young men in the near neighbourhood, not to mention the admiration of several others who weren't quite so eligible. Marianne's could fleck fiercely with grey when her temper rose, but her more equable and charitable sister, Clarissa, never deemed it necessary to display such unevenness of spirit.

La! In every way they looked the same. In height, face and figure, there was none who could separate them, and few enough of the local women who didn't feel a pang of jealousy when their proudly held, slimly drawn figures stepped out on to the ballroom floor at the local assemblies. But, Constance told herself gaily, there's no doubting which is which today.

And so it was. Clarissa's gown was old, well past its best and dowdy to a degree her twin sister would never tolerate for a moment. Its colour was a nondescript shade of brown, and it had, moreover, been overlaid with a soil-stained overall that might once have been described as white by a more charitable onlooker.

'I don't know how you can bear to wear that gown,' Marianne quizzed her. She raised her eyes to her sister's head and shuddered, 'and that old bonnet must have been long out of fashion when Aunt Constance was a young girl.'

'My hat may no longer be in the first flush of youth,' Clarissa conceded the point when she lifted a hand to its wide poke, 'but it's perfect for keeping the sun off my face while I'm at work.' Their voices matched to the very last inflection, just as their face and form.

'I don't know why you do,' replied Marianne with a stifled yawn. She eyed the flower-laden trug in her sister's arms with some amusement. 'Jarvis would have picked those blooms for you.'

'I enjoy working in the garden,' Clarissa returned calmly, 'and, as for the flowers, you know how Aunt Constance adores them.'

'Aunt Constance!' Marianne flung a baleful glance at the window where their aunt waited. She, too, dearly loved the woman who had looked after them both ever since she could remember, but nevertheless allowed that her aunt was old-fashioned and depressingly set in her ways. She flung her head back, allowing the pale pastel pinks of the painted silk scarf that held fast her wide brimmed straw chip hat to float on the air behind her.

Marianne hadn't enjoyed herself pottering about the garden like her more industrious sister. She'd taken a handful of the latest fashion plates down to the wide lawns and lounged in a comfortable seat while she pretended to examine them. In truth, she'd spent far more time in day-dreaming than in perusal of the fashions depicted. Her own preferences, were she ever allowed them, would lean more towards living the fashionable life than poring over illustrations, however exquisitely drawn.

'I'm sure Aunt Constance wouldn't have withheld her consent to our making up a party to the assembly rooms without good reason.' Clarissa knew exactly what ills Marianne had placed at their aunt's door. There was a grand ball due to be held in nearby St Neots that very week, but, to the dismay of both young girls, their aunt had vetoed the plan.

'Everyone we know will be there.' Marianne's voice rose in righteous indignation. 'Only dowds like us will miss it.'

Clarissa laughed out loud, charming her sister down from the boughs on the instant. 'Dowds indeed!' She stared long and hard at Marianne's modishly cut gown, a gay confection in the palest of pinks, and adorned with a plethora of bows and lace in the same sweet colour.

Marianne was abashed for no more than a moment. 'I still declare it's too much for us to miss such an event,' she offered up in complaint. Then, realizing she would make no headway against her sister's continued good humour, she stamped her feet in mock dismay and added a disconcerting rider, 'You're much too virtuous; surely the perfect match for our good rector.'

'Doctor Pym?' Clarissa failed to rise to the bait, though her sister had offered it many a time before.

'You know very well he's smitten with you, Clarissa,' Marianne twitted her sister at the rector's ardour. 'Mark my words, he'll make you an offer before the winter is through.'

'Oh, I do hope not,' Clarissa murmured. She found the young cleric an admirable young man, but far too intense for her sensibilities, though she'd never been known to snub him in the manner Marianne sometimes did.

'Don't be such a goose,' Marianne told her mirthfully. 'Every woman must wish to be married, and you two will deal very well together.' Her face fell when a sudden terrible thought struck her. 'I hope he doesn't mistake us and make his offer to me instead.' She recovered with a grin. 'I'll roast him if he does.'

Clarissa joined in her laughter, though in truth, she was more than a little wary that the good rector might indeed propose a union between the two of them.

'While you're engaged in good works with your husband, perhaps I'll be able to undertake a London season at long last.' Marianne's lips curved into a euphoric smile and a far-away look entered her eyes. 'I'd enjoy that more than anything, even if you wouldn't care to undertake such pleasurable and non-productive pastimes.'

'Oh, but I'd like it too,' confided Clarissa, looking more wistful than her twin had ever seen her.

'No!' Marianne's eyes were set wide on her sister's face. 'You've always disapproved of such a selfish existence as the fashionable ton enjoy. You know you have.'

'True enough,' agreed Clarissa, choosing her words carefully, 'but I can enjoy a measure of that life without indulging in its self-centred extremes. Besides, I should prefer to expand my horizon beyond country life before I'm wed.'

'To your virtuous rector,' Marianne baited her. They'd almost reached the rambling outline of the house and, when her gaze fell on her aunt once more, a curious glint lit up her eyes.

'I do believe Aunt Constance is holding a letter in her hands,' she told her sister, instantly relegating the subject of Clarissa's admirer to the back of her mind.

'Yes,' agreed that girl equably. 'The mail was delivered not more than an hour since.'

'Why didn't you say so at once?' Marianne clapped her hands together and gathered up her skirts to scamper in unladylike haste towards the door.

'It was addressed to Aunt Constance herself,' laughed Clarissa, hardly surprised that her impulsive twin should be so excited by such an event. 'I doubt if it's anything to do with us.'

'I don't believe it,' returned her twin excitedly. 'Aunt

Constance hardly ever receives a letter on her own account. Besides, she's waiting for us to join her.'

That their Aunt Constance, who had devoted her entire life to the twins' welfare, would often find herself waiting for the pair of them didn't occupy a significant part in Marianne's thoughts. Her aunt was awaiting them with a letter in her hand, and that event alone was enough to cause Marianne to expect a momentous happening, however often she'd been disappointed in the past.

She was to be thwarted again, however, for without giving any indication as to whether or not the contents of her letter affected her young wards, Aunt Constance sent them straight upstairs to dress for dinner. They kept country hours in Bedfordshire and would dine unfashionably early to their town cousins' eyes.

It wasn't until they were sitting quietly in the parlour digesting their dinner that Marianne's curiosity concerning the letter's contents was satisfied. Aunt Constance had given no sign of having the missive to hand during the meal, and even Marianne's impatience had balked at alluding directly to its existence without her aunt's permission. None the less she'd attempted to swing conversation that way on more than one occasion, only to be thwarted by an aunt who'd had more than a little experience of her niece's encroaching ways.

'I have a letter here,' Aunt Constance confessed at last, drawing the very article from a capacious pocket sewn into her gown. She paused a moment in search of her spectacles, then perched them precariously on her nose. 'It's from my sister, Eleanor.'

'Eleanor?' Marianne couldn't help the exclamation escaping her lips, and even the gentle Clarissa looked startled. Both girls knew of Aunt Eleanor's existence, though neither of them had ever met the lady, nor did they remember the last time she'd communicated with their guardian, if ever she had.

'As you know,' – Aunt Constance disregarded Marianne's ill-mannered outburst – 'your Aunt Eleanor made a good marriage to Mr Markham and moved to London while you were still quite young.' She didn't specify how young, but both Marianne and Clarissa realized they could have been little more than babies.

'I believe her entertainments are quite out of the common way,' continued their aunt, 'and that she enters enthusiastically into the life of the ton.' She paused to bestow a gentle smile on her charges. 'Which brings me to the contents of her epistle.'

'As you know, she has never been blessed with children herself, and though she's not been actively involved in your upbringing, I thought it fit to write to her regarding your circumstances.' She glanced up again and caught sight of two expectant faces. Rapt attention indeed, but she'd have to blight the hopes of one, at least. 'In short, she's agreed to sponsor one of you for the season in London.'

'One of us?' Marianne stared aghast at her aunt. 'Why can't she sponsor the pair of us? You know how well we deal together. Taking both of us would place no additional burden on her.'

'She's very specific, I'm afraid.' Constance balanced her spectacles on her nose and read verbatim from the letter in her hands: *'If that one takes, and there's no reason why she shouldn't unless she lacks the proper address, she may be married within the year and able to sponsor her sister herself.'* She allowed her eyes to dwell on the pair. 'You must remember that your Aunt Eleanor has no experience of daughters, nor indeed of any children. Both of you arriving together might very well prove too much of a responsibility for her to bear.'

'I should like to go.' Marianne spoke the words more to her sister than Aunt Constance, but it was that lady who answered.

'Clarissa is the elder by several minutes,' she reminded her niece gently. 'It should be her chance by right.'

'Please.'

Clarissa stared wide eyed at the tears already sparkling in her sister's eyes and capitulated. She had an idea she was being manipulated, but she loved her sister too much and, after all was said and done, her sibling wanted the position more than she.

'Marianne may go in my stead,' she told her aunt wistfully.

'Oh, thank you. Thank you.' Marianne threw her arms about her sister and tried to draw her into a dance of unashamed joy. Clarissa hung back, however, abashing even the lively Marianne, who suddenly understood how much it would have meant to her sister too. She hung her head for a moment, but was unable to restrain her joy for long.

'I'll make a brilliant marriage at once,' she vowed, 'and bring you out in such style that royalty themselves wouldn't be too high a touch for you.'

'Thank you, no,' declared Clarissa, laying her own disappointment to one side in the joy of her sister's good fortune. 'They're all fat old men and much too dissolute for my taste.'

'What about money?' Marianne began to tot up the cost of the clothes she would need and felt quite faint at the sums involved.

'Your father had his faults,' Aunt Constance told her with fine understatement, 'but that of penury cannot be laid at his door. The both of you may depend upon a respectable dowry to take into your marriage, and there are, in addition, adequate funds available for launching you into society.' She paused, making some calculations of her own. 'If we're careful, a few new purchases supplemented by prudent refurbishing of your best gowns will allow you to face society without fear of disgrace.'

'I have some savings set by, too,' Clarissa offered generously. 'Not enough to pay for new gowns, but ample for the purchase of a few folderols.'

'Thank you, Clarissa.' Aunt Constance's melting smile was more than adequate recompense for the girl. 'You're a most generous soul.'

'Oh, yes. Thank you.' Marianne showed signs of throwing herself on Clarissa's neck again, until Aunt Constance silenced them with a peremptory gesture.

'Please, girls,' she chided them. 'I have something further to tell you that won't wait.' She watched them anxiously while they settled down politely to listen. 'I should have made the whole known to you before, but the events leading up to this tale were as painful to me as they may prove to you, and the time never seemed right. Now you're on the brink of entering polite society, you'll have to know the truth of the matter.' She stared directly at Marianne. 'Especially you, my dear, though it impinges directly on both your lives.' She paused as though she didn't know how to start, then haltingly began to relate the painful tale.

'You may wonder,' she began, 'why it is that Eleanor, who is after all, both my sister and your aunt, never took a great deal of notice of our situation....'

'London is a long way off, Aunt.' Clarissa sensed her aunt's unease when that woman's voice trailed off. 'I doubt if Papa encouraged her to enquire after us either. He never had a good word to speak of Aunt Eleanor that I heard.'

'The story began with your parents' marriage.' Aunt Constance ignored Clarissa's interjection, although she knew it to be prompted by the best of motives. 'It was a union doomed from the start, though it may not have seemed that way to them during the first throes of love. Even when he was young, your father's character was serious to the point of asceticism, and he was moreover, a scholar, while your mother was the very opposite. She loved to dance, to sing, to hold and attend parties. Indeed, she thought and spoke of little else.'

As might be expected, Constance held the rapt attention of both her nieces. Their mother had passed away while they were still in swaddling clothes, and was rarely, if ever, mentioned.

'At first, your father was merely amused by her liveliness,' Constance continued. 'For a time, he even joined in her sport on occasions, a constant source of amazement to those of us who knew him well.' She shook her head wearily. 'It couldn't last for ever. Your father tired rapidly of the constant social round and began to tax your mother that she partook of such vulgar entertainment. On her part, she took no notice of his pleas, thwarting his every attempt to bring her to heel. Their heated arguments left Eleanor and I quaking sometimes, for his temper was never slow, but your mother, tiny as she was, stood up to him. She never showed any fear of his threats, even laughed in his face.'

'Did he kill her, then?' Marianne's eyes shone like saucers in her face at these revelations about her parents.

'No, child.' Aunt Constance wondered for a moment at the lack of filial feeling demonstrated by the girl, then turned to watch Clarissa's face. There was no emotion showing in that quarter either and she suddenly realized she might as well have been talking of strangers as their mother and father. The mother they had never known, and the father had always been such a remote, rather severe figure. Not that he had ever been unkind to the girls, or even stern. Really they might as well have been the servants' children for all the notice he had taken of them. They had still been young when he died too.

'When your mother fell pregnant, we all assumed she'd calm down and turn to providing a home for you and your father. We were soon forced to concede we were wrong and admit that, if anything, she had become wilder, almost uncontrollable. Indeed, your father believed she must have lost her reason, so frenzied were her escapades in society. Eleanor and I fell prey to her excesses, too, for all society appeared to look down on us as well as she. Then, at the last, Eleanor fell in love. Robert was by far the most handsome man any of us had ever seen and he soon began to pay court to Eleanor, wooing her with all the ardour a woman could long for.'

'Mr Markham?' Marianne's face held a rapturous smile at such a romantic tale. 'He sounds the most amiable of men.'

'So he is,' replied her aunt in coldly quelling tones. 'He is not, however, named Robert.'

'Oh. Then....' Marianne looked uncomfortable for a moment. She didn't understand. Had Aunt Eleanor married Robert or not?

'Do be quiet, Marianne,' put in her sister and turned again to her aunt. 'Please go on. Where do we come into this?'

'Robert and Eleanor were betrothed.' Aunt Constance swallowed hard, not at all anxious to relate such a disgraceful tale to her innocent young nieces.

'Please tell us.' Clarissa's face had taken on a deathly hue. It was almost as if she had already guessed.

'Only days before they were due to marry, Robert went off in the company of your mother. Somehow she'd wheedled her way into his affections and become his lover. She was, after all, quite extraordinarily pretty, and had a way of batting her eyes at a man until he could hardly be said to own his own soul.' She paused. 'Eleanor always blamed your father for her bride-groom's betrayal.'

'And he blamed her,' replied Clarissa quietly. 'That would be just like him.'

'Yes,' admitted Aunt Constance. 'He more or less threw my sister out of the house before he shut himself in his study for weeks on end. I believe he still loved your mother, or the woman she'd once been. Perhaps even the woman he wanted her to be, and never was. Whatever the reasons, he and Eleanor never spoke again, nor communicated in any other way. I even attended her wedding celebrations without his support.'

'Is that why he never loved us?' Clarissa's clear voice asked the question, but both girls were watching their aunt's face as carefully when she answered.

'I don't believe he ever went so far as hating you,' she reflected, 'but somehow he could never bring himself to think of you as children belonging to him. The full responsibility for your upbringing was laid on my shoulders from that moment.' She spoke simply. 'I tried to provide you with the love of both a mother who'd left and a father who couldn't.'

'And you succeeded.' Clarissa wound her arms around her aunt's shoulders. 'We never once missed either of them.'

'Will Aunt Eleanor dislike me too?'

'No, dear,' Aunt Constance reassured Marianne on that matter with a smile on her face. 'She never forgave your father for his cold indifference, but she forgot Robert long ago. Her marriage to Mr Markham might have been one of convenience in the first instance, but it's most certainly prospered since. Now your father's dead, she's ready to take over responsibility for you, and I'm sure she'll love you just as much as I do once you reside in her house and she gets to know you.'

'I wish Clarissa was coming with me.'

'You'll soon forget me,' prophesied her sister, 'when you're involved in the pleasures of the season.'

'And our poor life too,' added Aunt Constance, thankful the tale had been so easily accepted.

———•◦✦◦•———

CHAPTER TWO

Marianne's Letters

'Good afternoon and well met, Miss Meredew.' Doctor Pym addressed Clarissa warmly, approving, as always, of her industrious nature and sober good taste.

'Good afternoon, Rector.' Clarissa, while she greeted him politely, was simmering inside. She'd been meaning to address the pretensions of an awkward clump of nettles for several days, and following a light luncheon in the company of her aunt, she'd donned her oldest gown to complete the task. She might not hold the rector in any special regard, but, like most young ladies, she preferred not to be caught out in her dowdiest clothes. Neither did she wish to allow him any opportunity to declare himself, which, if she read the warning signs aright, he was in every danger of doing. Such a declaration would be an embarrassment to them both when her own feelings could not be engaged.

'I was meaning to take the air upon the Downs,' the cleric continued blandly, apparently unaware that the object of his desire was itching to rid herself of his company and return to her self-imposed task of decimating the nettle patch. 'When I saw you toiling so industriously, however, I was unable to prevent myself from approaching to express my admiration for your diligence.'

'Perhaps you'd like to take a turn, sir.' The girl waved her hand to indicate a further patch of the troublesome weed some little distance apart.

'I fear,' answered the rector with a polite smile, 'that I'm not properly dressed for the rigours of the garden.' He indicated a pair of pale pantaloons, half obscured by the dark frock coat he habitually wore.

Nor for the Downs so soon after a rainstorm, Clarissa decided, though she was too well mannered to point out that sentiment aloud. The rector, for whatever reason, had deliberately sought her out, and not just to compliment her on her skills in the garden.

'Miss Meredew.' The slightest of pauses. 'Clarissa!' Doctor Pym spoke her name with such sentiment that the girl could only gape at him. Oh, dear God, she panicked, he'll be down on one knee in a moment.

'I … we … we received another letter from Marianne this last weekend,' Clarissa began to gabble, petrified of the scene she was sure was about to be enacted. Oh, on my word, she wondered, why can't I deal with the rector in the same fashion I would the local squire's lad. She'd boxed his ears only a day or two before. Not that she wished to box the rector's ears, she acknowledged, merely to deal him a smart set-down.

The young squire's son hadn't been offering marriage, of course, but simply attempting to steal a sly kiss. Doctor Pym, to give him his due, would never have embarrassed her in that manner, though she wasn't sure that elevated his character above the common in her eyes. Where was the good in a lover who wouldn't make an attempt to kiss the one he loved? In any case, her feelings were as little taken by the cleric as his bolder neighbour, despite his worthy, not to mention religious, sincerity. Was it that very worthiness that held her hand from dealing with him in such a cavalier manner?

'Marianne?' Just as Clarissa had hoped the rector had been turned from his purpose by mention of her sister. In the heat of the moment he'd struggled for a moment to place the name, but a nice sense of propriety turned his purpose and made him ask after her. 'How is her visit to the metropolis continuing?' He began to reminisce in a prosy way over his own excursions in the nation's capital. 'I do hope she managed to find time to attend services in the Cathedral of St Paul. Its design is not considered universally popular, but I found it awe inspiring and a positive delight.'

'No indeed, I fear Marianne has not yet visited St Paul's.' Nor was she ever likely to, decided Clarissa, who had no intention of being drawn into the rector's recollections either. 'She has, I believe, made quite a successful entry into London society. You wouldn't believe the number of invitations she receives on a daily basis. I declare she could attend half-a-dozen entertainments every night of the week if she so chose.'

'I fear I'm unable to—'

'Mrs Markham is delighted with her reception by the ton,' Clarissa ruthlessly despatched the rector's attempt to interrupt her flow, 'and she's gained so many admirers I'm quite envious of her.'

'I cannot believe you'd ever envy your sister in such a regard.' There was a note of disapproval in the cleric's voice that began to arouse the girl's slow ire. 'You, I am sure, care not a whit for such frivolous pleasures. Surely you can conceive that I, that we—'

'Her most constant companion,' Clarissa cut in, before the rector could develop his theme, 'is Lord Leighton, who, from what she writes, appears to be wholly smitten and paying court to her. I am sure you must have come across him in your travels to the capital.'

'Indeed!' The cleric's colour had risen alarmingly, and the disapproval in his voice was beginning to show in his face. 'I never cared over much for the frivolous entertainments offered by society hostesses, though I was, of course, often included in their invitations. Thus I never met Leighton in person.' He shuddered theatrically. 'But I have heard stories of his exploits that would make your hair stand on end.'

'Really.' Clarissa stared at her hopeful swain with anticipation written clear across her face. The rector had turned red with embarrassment and there was an undertone of amusement bubbling though her voice that she made no attempt to disguise.

He evidently decided she didn't understand such matters and made an attempt to educate her. 'He is forever seeking out his own amusement without regard for the sensibilities of others. His days are spent in low haunts, frequented by boxers, drunks, beggars and the like, and he even partakes in such despicable activities himself.'

'He begs?' Clarissa could barely keep her laughter contained.

'No, indeed not. I only meant that he participates in such brutal sports as would be anathema to a high-born lady such as yourself.' The cleric, driven by his disapproval of such a lifestyle, went on. 'At night he will attend such dens of iniquity as the opera or the ballet before ending the evening in one of his clubs, gambling for high stakes until the early hours.'

'Is that all?' There was a faint note of disappointment in Clarissa's voice. Leighton, it seemed, was not so very far out of the ordinary amongst the London bucks. 'Marianne writes that he is considered most eligible amongst Aunt Eleanor's circle.'

'He has a title,' temporized the rector, 'and that alone is enough to raise the hopes of the matchmaking mamas of society. His estates are vast and they say he's as rich as Croesus, but I hope such worldly pretensions will not sway your sister's regard for his worth.'

'She writes that he pays her much attention, and surely the odd wager can't hurt. I myself have speculated at loo and even Aunt Constance has been known to lay the odd penny down at whist.'

'You are such an innocent, my dear Clarissa. Leighton does not bet in pennies, nor does he seek out women for any other reason than to ruin them. Marianne has far too lively a turn of mind for my liking, but it will surely prove her undoing if she encourages the advances of such a rake-hell.'

Clarissa bristled. She was not his dear, and neither did he have any right to criticize her sister. 'A rake-hell, sir?' She had the oddest feeling she wished to stamp her feet.

'I should not have sullied your delicate ears with such a term,' apologized the cleric immediately, 'but I couldn't remain silent on the matter when it so nearly affects your own dear self. Lord Leighton's scandalous amours are the talk of the Town.'

The normally even-tempered girl was left fuming over the rector's assumption of protection and may well have been goaded into delivering such a set down as Doctor Pym would have remembered for many a long day if her aunt had not suddenly appeared at the top of the garden.

'Clarissa, my dear,' she called out excitedly, 'we have not one, but two, letters delivered to the house and they are both addressed by Marianne for I recognize the handwriting.'

'You must excuse me, Rector.' In all common politeness Clarissa ought to have invited the cleric to take some refreshment with them, but she was still out of humour with the man.

'I'm sure you'll understand when I tell you we wish to learn Marianne's latest news immediately.'

'Of course. I'm taking up far too much of your valuable time. I'll say my goodbyes.' Doctor Pym found himself outmanoeuvred, with no other option left than to retire, but to soothe his sensibilities he added an arch and slightly pompous rider. 'We will speak again, Clarissa, and if I inform you that meeting must be undertaken in private, perhaps you can guess the reason.'

'Goodbye.' Clarissa turned and, catching up her skirts, ran nimbly towards her aunt, who was hurrying down the garden, before he could develop the theme any further.

As soon as the two ladies had comfortably seated themselves in the drawing-room overlooking the front of the house, Aunt Constance began to peruse the envelopes through her spectacles.

'This first letter is addressed to the both of us, my dear.' She adjusted her eye glasses to sit more comfortably on the bridge of her nose and began to break open the wafer. 'The other is addressed to you alone, though I cannot for the life of me think of anything she would wish to say that wouldn't concern myself as nearly as you.'

Clarissa smiled sweetly, but didn't elaborate. In all likelihood Marianne had embarked on some mad scheme that would throw their staid, maiden aunt into hysterics if she were to discover it. She'd read the letter out loud, of course; she knew how well Aunt Constance loved to receive news of her erstwhile charge. Some judicious editing of the contents might prove appropriate though.

'*My dearest Aunt and sweetest of Sisters,*' Aunt Constance began to read the missive out loud, frowning over the evident jumble of words. '*I have the most exciting news to impart. You will never guess, but Lord Leighton has made his offer to me. He is the most formal of men, several years my senior, and spoke first to my uncle to obtain his permission. Just as soon as she caught the gist of their conversation, though I had not the slightest idea he was even in the house, Aunt Eleanor escorted me to my room. There I put on the new white jacquard lace over a petticoat of the most subtle shade of pink with a full flounce all around the hem. She has proved the dearest of aunts and purchased several new gowns for me since my visit began, though she is sadly virtuous in the cut of their bodice. I am a positive dowd compared to some of my acquaintance and she insists on my wearing a modest chemisette during the day, even today of all days. Only think how foolish that must seem when Lord Leighton was to ask me to be his bride.*

'Mr Markham, the most amiable of men, escorted me to his study where he left me alone with Leighton, though I should now in all conscience call him Richard. I was shy at first, but he spoke most eloquently and conducted himself just as he should. Only think how pink my face became when he dropped to one knee and asked me to be his bride. As you can imagine I clapped my hands with glee and told him I would be honoured. Aunt Eleanor tells me I should be very happy with my conquest for he is the greatest prize imaginable. I am pleased, of course; all my new friends will be pea-green with envy.'

Aunt Constance looked up with shining eyes. 'My little baby,' she began, 'is to be married.'

'To Lord Leighton.' Clarissa's face reflected her feelings.

'Yes, child.' Aunt Constance stared at her troubled niece, wondering what was so untoward with her.

'I was just this minute speaking with Doctor Pym.' Her voice trailed off, unsure of how she should continue when she was already half aware that the rector's aversion to Leighton was driven by his own considerations on what constituted worth in a man.

'I saw him leave. What of it?' Constance's face suddenly assumed a quizzical look. 'He didn't offer for you?'

'No, Aunt.' Clarissa grinned. 'Not for the want of trying, but I should die of boredom within a se'enight were I to wed him.' She paused to gather her thoughts. 'He spoke of Leighton of whom he had some knowledge. I dare say gambling, even for high stakes, is commonplace for a man of his means, but he seems to waste all his talents in the pursuit of pleasure and Doctor Pym hinted that he was also a most notorious rake.'

'I should pay the rector no attention, my dear. No doubt Leighton, like most young men, will have set up liaisons with girls from the opera or the ballet. He may even have kept a mistress; some men do, you know. But you may depend on it that such a practice will end when he marries.'

'Marianne will sometimes lead a man on with her flirting,' Clarissa offered, astounded that her staid aunt could speak so off-handedly of mistresses and the like. She understood such practices were commonplace amongst the fashionable young bucks of the ton, and had even held whispered, slightly shocking, conversations with Marianne on the subject. But Aunt Constance? 'You don't suppose he will think my sister is some-what less than the innocent she is, and only pursues her to add to his trophies?'

'Leighton would not be made welcome in society if he made a practice of seducing innocent young girls of his own class. Neither would he ask the girl to marry him if that were his aim. No doubt he's been made aware of his responsibilities; such a man must possess an heir to carry on the family line.'

'What about love?'

'To be in love with the man you marry may be the ideal, but hardly the norm in society. I'm sure Leighton's attracted to Marianne. What man wouldn't be? She's well born and a beauty to boot, but a man like him, who can take his pick from the flower of society, will be looking for a wife to enhance his position and bear him heirs. Very likely their regard will grow comfortably with the years, just like that of Eleanor and Mr Markham. After all, your sister is hardly mooning after the man herself. In the letter she describes her costume with more animation than her husband to be.'

'I wonder what Marianne is really thinking?' Clarissa sighed, faintly disappointed to find her bubble burst. Perhaps she should settle for the rector after all. She paused to think. No, that would be going too far.

'Of her trousseau, I don't doubt.' Aunt Constance thought a moment before she changed the subject. 'I dare say Eleanor will invite us to stay with her for the ceremony. We must think of refurbishing our own wardrobes. I wonder how long Leighton will want Marianne to himself before she may present you to the ton. Since she has taken so well, it follows that you must too, since you are as alike as two peas in a pod.'

'I doubt if I'll make such a brilliant marriage, but perhaps a respectable one, Aunt.' Nor would I want to, Clarissa decided. In her heart and in her dreams she still hoped for a love match. Was that such an impossible dream in the world of fashion? She was usually categorized as the sensible one of the pair, but she'd always held on to her secret dreams of love. 'Is there no more to read, Aunt?' She returned to the letter.

Constance skimmed through the balance of the missive quickly, too excited by the unexpected news to read it verbatim. 'Most of the remainder is commonplace,' she complained. 'Leighton has other commitments to honour and will be gone from Town for most of the month to tour his estates, after which the engagement will be formally announced at a ball the Markhams are throwing in honour of the couple.' She looked up and spoke directly to her niece. 'I believe his properties to be vast.' She scanned the words again. 'Only think, they are situated in several parts of the country.' She shrugged. 'You can read the whole later. There may be more to the point in your own letter.'

Clarissa broke the seal and held up the close-written missive. 'It is dated several days following your letter,' she said.

'Mr Markham is a Member of Parliament, but I believe he generally has his letters franked by his sponsor, the duke. No doubt he is a busy man and his availability may have an adverse effect on their delivery,' her aunt explained. 'What does she have to say?'

Clarissa quickly scanned the document, dismayed to find her sister had penned no more than a short note to update her. There was nothing in it that her aunt could disapprove of.

'Leighton squired Marianne to no more than one party,' she summarized, 'before he left to inspect his estates. Otherwise she seems to be caught up in the usual round of gaiety.' She frowned. 'Apparently Lord Dalwinton has been pursuing her also. Too hotly for her comfort, she writes.'

'What?' exclaimed her aunt. 'Is that old roué still on the loose?'

Clarissa opened her eyes wide. 'Do you know him?'

'Of him, at least. He is the most contemptuous of men. An evil lecher, though I never heard of him attaching himself to a lady of virtue before. He ought to know better than chase an innocent young girl like Marianne at his age.'

Clarissa screwed up her eyes and concentrated on her sister's letter which had been crossed and re-crossed to reduce the postage. 'His attentions, though unwelcome, have become very marked,' she decided, wondering just what had happened. *'Since the engagement must remain our secret for the present, I have no one to rely on for protection until Leighton returns from his estates. Most fortunately for me a young officer on leave from the Continent intervened when Dalwinton caught me alone and attempted to kiss me. Leighton himself could not have dismissed his pretensions so well, nor struck such a well-chosen blow, all the while bravely dismissing his opponent's vengeful threats.'* Clarissa frowned again while she attempted to decipher the jumble of words. *'I have met Stephen on several occasions since and he is the most unexceptionable of young men, well received by all the hostesses of the ton.'* She looked up at her aunt with a grin. 'It seems Marianne has made another conquest. I hope Leighton will not be jealous.'

'Is that a visitor on the drive?' Aunt Constance may have complained that her hearing was failing on more than one occasion, but she could still detect the rustle of gravel under the wheels of a carriage. She leaned forward to peer out of the window.

'Yes,' she confirmed. 'I wonder who could be visiting unannounced at this time.'

Clarissa joined her at the window in time to watch one of the grooms place a wooden step under the carriage door. Aided by its presence, a slim, well-dressed lady of fashion alighted.

'Good gracious,' Constance exclaimed. 'It's Eleanor.'

CHAPTER THREE

Aunt Eleanor

'Well, I declare.' Aunt Eleanor strode angrily into the drawing-room in the wake of the housekeeper who'd answered her peremptory knock and straight away confronted her niece. 'So you are here, madam. A fine way you have of repaying my hospitality after all I've done for you. And as for you!' Eleanor turned to her sister, Constance. 'How could you allow Marianne to desert me in such a detestable fashion, and with her ball already arranged? I don't doubt half the town have discovered she's promised to Leighton and will be sniggering behind my back if she fails to attend her own betrothal.

'And Leighton!' Eleanor turned quite pale when she considered the successful swain. 'Let me tell you he is a proud and powerful man, who will undoubtedly set out to ruin us all if we succeed in making him the object of ridicule.' The lady faced Clarissa again, quite ignoring the amazement plain on the face of both ladies. 'I won't have it, and so I tell you, young lady. Go and find your pelisse immediately. How far we can travel when it is already late in the day I don't know, but I cannot stay another moment in the house of my sister, not when she could condone such a treacherous outrage.'

'What are you talking about, Eleanor?' Constance had turned quite pale under the indignant barrage, but the flags were beginning to fly in her cheeks. She remembered how Eleanor had always been ready to blame her younger sister for the veriest of trifles, and, for all the world, it seemed as though the leopard had failed to change its spots through the long years of separation.

'What am I talking about?' There was outrage in Eleanor's voice. 'Marianne stands unashamedly in front of us and you have to ask me what I'm talking about. Get yourself ready to leave right now, girl.'

'Please, Aunt Eleanor.' Clarissa spoke up, realizing her aunt was talking at cross-purposes. 'I am not Marianne, but her twin sister, Clarissa.' She paused while the other stared at her. 'We really are very alike in looks.'

Eleanor was struck dumb for a moment, but she rallied swiftly. 'I don't believe you for a moment,' she declared, but there was a look of reassessment in her eyes that told the truth. She might not have been completely convinced, but much of the wind had been taken from her sails.

'Nevertheless, it's true.' Constance took up the battle, only to be ruthlessly interrupted by her elder sister.

'Then where is Marianne?' The question started stridently, but wallowed into a wavering acceptance. 'Is she truly not with you?' Eleanor seized hold of Constance's hands, a stricken look upon her face.

'No, Aunt, she is not,' Clarissa cut in with a worried frown. 'We should rather ask the question of you. Have you come to inform us she is missing?'

'Marianne missing? No, of course not.' Eleanor's face crumpled. 'Only I don't know where she can be.'

'Come, Eleanor.' A concerned-looking Constance took up the challenge. 'Either you know where she is, or you don't.'

'I suggest you make yourself comfortable and tell us the story from the beginning.' Clarissa was as worried as either of her aunts, but she could see that Eleanor was close to dissolving into hysterics. 'Come, let me help you out of your outdoor clothes and I'll arrange for a drink to be brought through for you. Brandy would seem appropriate in the circumstances.'

'I believe I'll have one too.' Constance collapsed into an easy chair, mopping her brow with a lace handkerchief she'd retrieved from her pocket.

In any other circumstance Clarissa would have admired the flowing lines of the yellow jean pelisse matched with half boots in the same material and quite set off by the Russian bonnet perched atop her aunt's head. As it was she flung the garment loosely across a convenient stool and called for their house-keeper to fetch the reviving brandy immediately.

'Now, Aunt,' she began, 'tell us the whole and start from the beginning. What has happened to Marianne? I gather she's left your protection, but have you any idea where she's gone? Or why?'

Eleanor sank back into the chair she had been offered and sighed faintly. 'Oh my dears,' she began her account, 'I don't know where to begin.'

'Leighton is not involved?' Clarissa was still wary of that gentleman's alleged rakish tendencies, and her Aunt Eleanor's fear of what his proud and imperious nature might induce him to do to the family in order to revenge himself hadn't abated her trepidation one iota.

'Oh no, my dear. Only think he left to inspect his estates some two or three weeks ago, and hasn't been seen in Town since. Marianne's spirits appeared to change after he left, though. At first she was aglow with pride and excitement in securing such a catch, but lately she has been cast down. I didn't pay it any mind at first, she was missing Leighton perhaps. But, on reflection, that couldn't have been the reason. Marianne isn't the kind of girl to mope, and in any case they had met so very little before she was promised.'

'Were they in love?'

'Of course they were,' Aunt Eleanor reassured Clarissa brightly. 'Who could not love Marianne and, as for Leighton, why, he is the biggest prize on the marriage market.'

'He squired her to a party before he left to inspect his estates? Marianne wrote something of it.'

'Yes. I did wonder if he'd crowded his fences with her that evening and made a note to talk to her after the Farthingales' party.'

'Crowded his fences?'

A delicate blush tinged Eleanor's face. 'I wondered if he might have frightened her.' She broke off at the look on her niece's face. 'I'm sorry, my dear, you are so very young and innocent, but I must be blunt. He may have tried to make love to her.'

'Make love to her?'

'A kiss, a cuddle. The sort of thing any girl with a bit of town bronze to her would make light of, particularly in the case of the man she was betrothed to.' Eleanor paused to correct herself. 'Not that any young girl of breeding would allow a man to whom she was not promised to act in such a manner.' Her voice began to register disapproval. 'He should have recognized Marianne was only a country maid, however well she'd conducted herself in Town. Damn him, he should have known how to go on with her. She was apprehensive, and that is understandable, but there is not the slightest need. Leighton is, after all, a gentleman.' She stopped to compose herself again, allowing Clarissa to set her to the right.

'Quite what Leighton's idea of love-making might be, I can have no notion,' she declared forthrightly, 'but Marianne would not have fallen into the mopes over a kiss and cuddle. Very likely she'd have been all the more disappointed if he didn't try something of the sort.' Clarissa vividly remembered how she'd found her headstrong sister calmly kissing their dance instructor one afternoon. A mere experiment, or so she'd declared, but Marianne had been neither set down, nor apologetic over that incident!

'So Markham assured me, but that is why I speculated she might have posted back home to you. Only now I am quite out of ideas, and quite out of patience with the chit.'

'Out of patience.' Clarissa rarely lost her temper, but she came close to slapping the silly woman sitting in front of her. 'Marianne has disappeared, and you are out of patience with her?'

'That's what is so strange about the whole affair,' Eleanor chimed in, feeling calmer now she'd rid herself of her irritation. 'She is gone and I have to admit I don't know where, but she hasn't entirely disappeared. We received a note from her on the following day.'

'Are you sure it was from her?'

'No doubt about it. I'd know her handwriting anywhere. She wrote such pretty letters for me.' Eleanor spread her hands wide in a gesture of resignation. 'It was the day after the Farthingales' party and I was abed until late morning.'

'Did Marianne attend the party too?'

'She was expected to, but I received word she was to travel with a party of her friends.' Eleanor hung her head. 'I didn't know it then, but that was a lie, for those very friends missed her too. All I knew at the time was that I didn't see her at the Farthingales', though it was such a squeeze it would be easy to miss one young person in all the throng.' She paused to explain. 'I had the most dreadful headache and left the party early in company with Markham. Little did we realize what our ungrateful niece was planning.

'Next morning, later on as I explained, Marianne's own maid passed me the note. It was most definitely in Marianne's hand-writing, but it gave us no clue to her whereabouts. It said only that we were not to worry for her and that she would return as soon as she was able.'

'Where did the maid find the note?'

'That is what's so odd about it. Marianne gave the note to her in person. She'd packed herself a portmanteau and left the house early that very morning, yet I'll swear she hadn't been in her room the previous evening. I heard from the housekeeper herself that Marianne's bed hadn't been slept in. Whatever tipped the scales happened the previous evening, but it can have nothing to do with Lord Leighton.'

'Has the maid been in your employ for long?'

'Three or four years, as I remember,' Eleanor confirmed. 'She followed her mother into service.'

'Then she is entirely trustworthy?'

'A servant can never be trusted completely for they will rob you blind if they think they can get away with it.' Eleanor showed her prejudices. 'But Sophie was elevated from under-stairs to take on the role of maid to your sister. She was utterly devoted to her mistress, and I don't doubt her word on this matter. The note, I am sure, was left by Marianne.'

'Have you informed the Runners?'

'Of course not. Only think what a to do that would cause. The girl left of her own free will, even left us a note saying she'd be back. If we had some clod hopper about us playing detective word would soon be all around the ton. Marianne would be the subject of the most scandalous *on-dits*, and we'd all be ruined. The disgraceful behaviour of her mother would be spread abroad again too. Like mother, like daughter; they'd all be saying it behind her back.'

'She couldn't have found our mother, could she?'

'No, of course not.' Eleanor stared at her sister and when that woman gave a nod continued with her explanation. 'Your mother's long dead, child. Once she'd run off with Robert they were no longer accepted in polite circles and straight away posted off to the more liberal surroundings of Paris. They were never married, never could be whilst your father was alive, and Robert was cut off from his family's fortune. They borrowed heavily and eventually Robert left her to face their creditors alone. I heard, years later, that she died in abject poverty.' She sighed heavily. 'There's no doubt that this disappearance, if discovered, will ruin your sister's reputation and yours too, very like.'

'What did you tell her friends?' Clarissa didn't care a fig for her reputation, nor for the fate of a mother she'd never known, not when her beloved sister was missing.

'Only that Marianne had contracted a chill and must not venture out for a while. We hoped she'd soon reappear, but when her friends began to call on us, we had to pretend she'd posted to her Aunt Constance's cottage in the country to recuperate.' Eleanor nodded in satisfaction. 'That's what made it so easy for me to visit without tongues wagging. Mark you, once the gossips have the measure of our discomfort, tongues will begin to wag.'

Suddenly the woman poked an accusing finger in Clarissa's direction. 'Wait,' she cried, staring at her niece as though she'd had a brain-wave. 'You look as alike as two peas in a pod. Your voices are identical too. Even once you introduced yourself I was still half convinced you were Marianne herself.' She turned to stare at her own sister. 'Clarissa must take her sister's place in our household. She can play the girl to perfection. Leighton will return to Town next week and our grand ball is imminent. It is imperative that Marianne is available to greet him.'

'But if Marianne plans to return?'

'It would be inconvenient to have two Mariannes in the game I don't doubt, but we could spirit you away on the instant. Markham shall arrange that much. He is sadly discomforted, poor man.'

'How can I play such a part when she is betrothed?'

'That is precisely why you must play the part. Marianne will lose her chance at marriage if she is suspected of running off. With the unfortunate example set by her mother, it is not only Leighton who will spurn her, but every other man with any pretension to a place in society. And don't expect any help from me if that happens. Markham and I will be the butt of every wag in Town if the girl we sponsored walks out, and Leighton will be the first to aid and abet them. The engagement is nothing while it is still an understanding, but Marianne must take her place at his side when we announce their betrothal at our grand ball.'

'Lord Leighton,' Clarissa issued the name faintly, 'is planning to marry her and will surely recognize I'm not the same girl to whom he plighted his troth.'

'My dear, you can take my word for it. Leighton doesn't know the chit so well he could tell you apart. At the best he squired her to parties, always in company, and even if they could have arranged a lover's tryst, and trust me they couldn't, they wouldn't have been left alone for long. Besides, he has been occupied on his estates for most of the month.'

'Was he not in love with her?'

'Of course not. It is a marriage of convenience on his part, though no doubt he made sure he could both like and admire her. He needs an heir and therefore a wife. Marianne was the current beauty, hailed everywhere as a *nonpareil*. Surely a man such as he would take nothing less, especially when he discovered her nature was as sweet as her face.'

'What if he tried to make love to me?' Clarissa's face ran red when she imagined the scene.

'Pooh.' Her aunt scoffed at her fears. 'If you truly love your sister then you must dismiss his pretensions on that score or kiss him back. He's a handsome man with some little experience from all that's been said. It shouldn't be such an arduous task after all.'

Clarissa wasn't so sure as her aunt, but she had begun to realize she might be her sister's only hope for future happiness. Marianne of all people would have no wish to lose her place in society, and at Leighton's side she would be at the very head of it. She would do all in her power to retain that dream for her sister.

Her head began to spin. The devil take her sister. Where was Marianne? Why had she left Aunt Eleanor's protection? There seemed no answer to these questions, which only raised them higher in Clarissa's mind.

Was she lost? That didn't fit, not if she'd packed her own portmanteau and left a note with her maid. Clarissa made a note to get hold of that missive. It was all very well for Aunt Eleanor, who'd known Marianne for no more than a couple of months, to declare it wasn't a forgery, but she knew her sister's handwriting better than anyone.

In hiding? Where? All those whom Marianne knew in the metropolis were of their rank, and surely none of her society friends would offer her shelter when they knew she was in the care of the Markhams. It wasn't as though they were monsters. And what was she hiding from? Clarissa's mind was more surely set on that detail. Lord Leighton was easily cast as the villain who'd frightened her away.

Kidnapped? No, she couldn't have been, or there would been a ransom note by now, unless she was to be sold in some sleazy eastern bazaar, a fate the heroine of one lurid novel they'd read in secret had suffered. In any case there was a note, a note that purported to herald her return, unless Marianne had been forced to write it. The sisters had once read a novel in which that very thing had happened. The hero had intervened in a later chapter, of course, but there would be no hero for Marianne to fall back on.

Leighton too, Clarissa reasoned, must be high on the list of suspects. He was just the sort of arrogant villain as the most dramatic of novels portrayed, the very man who would prey on the virtue of innocent young girls. Nevertheless, she determined bravely, I'll find Marianne if I have to search every building in the capital.

'I'll do it,' she declared out loud for the benefit of her aunts.

─◦◦◦─

CHAPTER FOUR

The Markham Household

Fortunately Constance and Clarissa lived at no great distance from London and, with an early start and a fortunate wind, Aunt Eleanor's coach ate up the miles. They stopped at noon for a nuncheon of thin sliced cold beef and freshly baked bread, served with a light wine which Eleanor declared to be particularly good for travelling on, despite her thinly veiled suspicion of rural coaching houses and the cleanliness of their kitchens.

A change of horses soon saw them trotting briskly towards the capital again and, freshly provisioned, Aunt Eleanor deigned to answer some of Clarissa's most urgent questions. The servants, surely Marianne would know them all, despite Aunt Eleanor's pleas to the contrary. At the very least her own maid and those commonly seen about the house would know her. Markham himself even. Clarissa shivered in dreadful fear that she would seize on an innocent visitor to the house and immediately expose her own deception by warmly greeting him as her uncle. Her friends! Aunt Eleanor's descriptions of these were sketchy at best and concerned more with their family and connections than the interests they had in common, and what else they might reasonably be expected to talk about.

She hadn't even raised the subject of Leighton, and Clarissa's spirits, which hadn't been buoyant to start with, began to sink further with every mile passed, despite the spate of amusing *on-dits* with which Aunt Eleanor attempted to regale her. In the end, all the girl felt she could hope for was not to be caught impersonating her sister within the first few minutes of arrival. Eleanor had no such worries on her mind: Clarissa was so much like Marianne, no one could possibly guess at their deception.

The vast urban sprawl of the metropolis began to intrude on them following the last change of horses at High Barnet and the long run across the common. This was a notorious haunt of highwaymen, and left Aunt Eleanor jittery, for by then, although it was still far from dark, the sun was beginning to sink lower in the sky. Villages began to come and go with ever increasing rapidity until they reached Islington, where the boundaries between one group of houses and the next became so blurred as to be barely discernible.

Clarissa's nose, attuned to the fresher pastures of the countryside, began to wrinkle in distaste when they passed through the poorer suburbs. Ramshackle jumbles of houses, many of them no better than byres, lined the narrow streets, with filth-strewn and noisome alleyways burrowing deep into their depths, their interiors too dark for the girl to even distinguish. The richer quarters of the merchant set's fine houses, walled around, formed almost a separate enclave in the midst of the foul smells and rotting odour of the poorer streets. The traffic, too, began to increase. So many wagons and carts of all kinds of trade, drawn by a positive miscellany of animals, and occasionally interspersed by the stylish equipage of the gentry, many of whom lifted their hats politely towards their own vehicle. Clarissa began to feel quite overcome by all the bustle and noise.

Then, finally, the capital began to show its more fashionable side. The streets were much broader, sometimes even paved; the houses somehow grander, even those barely larger than the simple cottages in her own village. Clarissa, at the last, shook off her blue mood and began to thrill to the thought of living in the midst of such fashionable society.

The Markhams' own London residence was situated at the heart of an elegant crescent, its pale stucco façade staring out over the wide expanse of manicured parkland that adjoined the opposite side of the street. The imposing door swung open almost as soon as both ladies had alighted from their vehicle and Clarissa stared up at the huge and magnificently dressed individual waiting at the head of the steps. Although unused to quite such magnificently attired servants, she decided it could only be the Markhams' butler, and strode up the steps to greet him.

'Downing,' she began, her heart leaping into her throat at the chance she was taking. 'How nice to see you again.'

'Miss Marianne.' Downing, for it was indeed the butler she addressed, inclined his head politely, as though his own consequence was scarcely less than hers. 'I trust your health is fully restored, miss, and may I assure you that the entire household are pleased to see you back where you belong.' He turned ponderously and addressed a lad dressed as a footman. 'Edward,' he admonished him with a quick wave of his hand.

Edward evidently understood his superior better than Miss Meredew for he scuttled down the steps to offer an arm to Eleanor, though Clarissa could scarcely believe her aunt needed his aid to ascend the steps.

'Uncle John.' A tall, fashionably dressed man appeared at the top of a wide staircase and she ran up to greet him with a kiss on one cheek as she was persuaded Marianne would have done.

'Marianne.' John Markham looked startled, as well he might in the circumstances. With secrecy at the forefront of her mind, Eleanor hadn't thought to warn her husband that Marianne was still missing and Clarissa was to play her part. Neither could he have guessed at the startling resemblance between the two sisters, when even his spouse had not known it.

'Where is Sophie? I must change from these clothes.' Clarissa had learned enough of Marianne's maid to know that the girl was in her confidence and would surely be her sister's first port of call, more especially when she'd been cooped up in a carriage for the best part of the day. In Clarissa's case, since it was patently obvious Markham knew nothing of their deception, a retreat to the privacy of her own room was even more imperative, when it would present Eleanor with the chance to update her husband.

'I had hoped to talk to you before dinner, Marianne.'

Clarissa could see the storm clouds gathering on her uncle's face, and realized he intended to read the girl he supposed to be her sibling a well-deserved scold for running away.

'Please, Uncle,' she pleaded. 'I will explain everything, but first let me wash away the grime of the road.'

Markham nodded, his face softening under the coaxing glance offered by his niece. 'Very well, puss. Go up to your room. Edward will send Sophie to attend you on the instant.'

Fortunately Aunt Eleanor had coached her well in the disposition of the house, and Clarissa set off up a further flight of stairs with her confidence restored. Evidently she'd fooled everyone so far and acted just as she ought. Sophie, from all she'd been told, knew her sister better and might be more difficult to deal with, but if she stuck to her aunt's story of a terrible sickness, then she hoped to thwart her maid's suspicions too. Any misgivings the girl had would have to remain just that, for Clarissa knew she was like enough in looks to Marianne to fool even the closest of servants.

'Miss Marianne?'

Clarissa stared at the pretty young girl who was standing quietly near the top of the stairway. Her eyes were wide as saucers and she looked as though she'd seen a ghost.

'Miss Marianne?' The girl tried again louder. Then, with a squeal of delight, launched herself headlong at Clarissa.

'Sophie.' Clarissa regarded the lass charging towards her with amusement until some sixth sense urged her to hold out her arms. Sophie, for such she most evidently was, flung herself into the embrace, and straight away began to pull her along the corridor.

'Oh Miss Marianne, I hardly thought to see you again so soon.'

'Please, Sophie,' Clarissa gasped. 'Not so fast, I'm still recovering my strength. Why I hardly recognize my own chamber.' That was no lie, for, despite Eleanor's description of the house, she'd been ill prepared for the number of doors opening off the corridor.

'Don't fun with me, Miss Marianne, there's no one else within hearing.' The girl threw open a door and ushered her in. 'How came you with Mrs Markham?'

'She brought me here in her carriage. Oh, it is heaven to be back.'

'So I should think when I consider what you must have endured. How is the patient?'

'I am well now, Sophie, and so glad to see you. Aunt Constance is dreadfully set in her ways, but that isn't such a bad thing when you're suffering.' Clarissa wiped her hand theatrically across her brow and hoped Aunt Constance would forgive her misrepresentations. She knew just how Marianne would have behaved in such circumstances.

'You've never worn that gown in public?' Sophie stared suspiciously at Clarissa's dress when she slipped out of her pelisse.

'I have.' The girl stared down at her clothing; perfectly respectable, but as she suddenly realized, not so dashing as Marianne would ordinarily wear at home, let alone in Town. She attempted to recover herself in the other's eyes, which were already clouding with suspicion. 'Aunt Constance would have me dress so. Help me out of it immediately.'

'I'll have a bath prepared for you.' Sophie pulled on a bell rope before she helped Clarissa to remove her gown. 'Here.' There was a polite rap on the door as the maid handed her a delightfully embroidered wrap, which she shrugged herself into while Sophie went to instruct someone on the other side of the door.

'Come through to the bedroom,' Sophie continued, leading her mistress through to the inner sanctum, 'and I'll dress your hair.'

'No.' Clarissa made the decision on the instant. 'Uncle John will wish to see me first.' Sophie's manner had changed and she realized the maid had become suspicious of her. But of what? And why? She shook her head wearily, she had no idea. Was it something she'd said? Or something she'd left unsaid? Or merely the way she was dressed? If only she knew how far the girl was in Marianne's confidence she might have rectified the omission. 'Have hot water made ready and I'll bathe as soon as I return,' she decided at last.

The next few days saw Clarissa settle comfortably into the household. For the most part it was a pleasurable existence, and if it hadn't been for her sister's continued absence, she would have enjoyed herself immensely. As it was, she found herself constantly searching for clues to Marianne's whereabouts, though she soon discovered how difficult it was to make enquiries about the movement of the very person she herself was impersonating.

Markham had nearly suffered an apoplexy when he heard the truth of the deception, but Eleanor soon brought him to see how necessary such a contrivance was, especially when he could see for himself how alike the two girls were. He huffed and puffed, but eventually owned that Clarissa would very likely pass as her sister. Then, to her immense relief, he tutored her for much of the following morning on the people she would be most likely to meet, especially her particular friends, whom he categorized as a particularly harum-scarum set. He also showed her the note Marianne had left.

The writing, though hurriedly scrawled, undoubtedly belonged to her sister, but the brief communication, as Aunt Eleanor had implied, did little to encourage her. '*My dearest Aunt Eleanor,*' she began to read aloud as though that would provide a further clue. '*I must leave your protection for the present, but you are not to worry unduly since I am comfortably situated and will return as soon as I am able. My fondest love, Marianne.*' There was no sign the missive had been written under duress, but no sign it hadn't either.

Eleanor took her part too, cancelling engagements under the pretext of Marianne's continued rehabilitation. 'We'll reintroduce you gradually into society,' she told Clarissa. 'Colonel Rodney, a close friend of your uncle, has seen fit to hold a select party for his daughters. Marianne knew them only slightly, for they are not yet fully out and much younger than the most of your friends.' She corrected herself, slightly self-consciously.

'Marianne's friends.' Then went on to warn the girl. 'It is a select occasion, but it is only fair to tell you that Emily, Marianne's closest companion, will attend also. If you can convince her of your authenticity, your role will be established.'

Sophie, also, continued to minister to her, unfailingly polite, but to the girl's overwrought senses suspicious also. Following her first ecstatic greeting, the maid did not display any further hint of affection above the norm, nor were any shared secrets let out, though Clarissa dug as deeply as she dared. For all their sakes, and especially Marianne's ambitions, she could not reveal her identity to the girl just because she was suspicious. There was no more than a forlorn hope the maid might know of her sister's whereabouts, but by all accounts the girl was devoted to Marianne and would surely have come forward herself if she suspected her mistress was in any trouble. No, let the girl hold her suspicions; she could have no inkling of the real truth.

Clarissa wouldn't have been human if she hadn't been excited by the impending visit to Colonel Rodney's. It was, after all, her first engagement in London, and though the party might seem tame, considering the age of the host's daughters, to one more used to the entertainments in the capital, she herself was in raptures. The fly in the ointment seemed likely to take the shape of Marianne's closest confident, Emily Paymount, and with a forthrightness typical of the girl, she insisted on meeting her supposed friend alone prior to the engagement. Better to be discovered in the deception in the privacy of the Markhams' home, than in the full glare of society. A sentiment that Markham concurred with fully.

Emily made the dreaded visit with her mother on the afternoon of the day preceding the Rodneys' gathering. At first the two girls sat close by the older women, uttering no more than the most common-place of greetings. Both visitors asked politely after Marianne's health, but it wasn't long before Mrs Paymount was discussing the latest scandalous *on-dit* to affect the ton with her hostess and, while their elders were gossiping, Clarissa was able to draw her sister's friend towards a cosy seat in the window, out of earshot.

'La, Marianne,' Emily began with an arch smile, 'I'm so pleased to see you well. Life has been so dreary these past few weeks without you in Town. You were always up to the latest rigs and tricks.' And then in an abrupt *volte-face*, 'What do you think to my new morning gown?' It was to be presumed that Marianne's thoughts were of no particular consequence for the girl continued without a trace of a pause, 'I shall wear the lilac to the Rodneys' party, of course. You remember the gown I mean, I modelled it last time I saw you.' She simpered knowingly. 'It's cut delightfully low and will fetch the most admiring glances.'

'Yes, indeed.' Clarissa's reply was so brief as to be insipid and Emily stared solicitously at her friend.

'Marianne,' she murmured, with some concern, 'I never thought to see you in the mopes. Are you sure you'll be recovered enough to attend the Rodneys' affair? There is very little chance of it proving to be a squeeze.' The girl began to stare at Clarissa with more solicitude than she'd shown previously.

'Oh, yes. I'm looking forward to attending.' There was more animation in Clarissa's reply this time, enough for Emily to be satisfied at any rate. 'Fanny and Jane are such delightful girls, I hear.'

'As to that, I couldn't say,' returned Marianne's friend in slightly bored accents. 'I barely know them. Fanny will be out later this year, I understand, but Jane is still in the schoolroom.

Their mother is such a dowd too; I dare say they'll turn out to be prim and proper, just like her. The party will no doubt prove insipid; there's no more than a handful invited.' Emily had returned to her air of world-weary sophistication, no doubt all the rage in fashionable circles.

'I'm glad you'll be there to liven it up then.' Clarissa felt she should add something to the conversation. 'Remember this will be my first function in over three weeks.'

'Oh, Marianne.' Emily reached out her hand and clasped Clarissa's arm considerately. 'I keep forgetting. You must have been dreadfully ill to retire to the country.'

'You can have no idea.' That much, at least, was true. 'Doctor Tynforde could not attend himself, but he sent his locum, only a young man, who straight away told Aunt Eleanor that I should need complete rest. Aunt Constance's house in the country was perfectly situated. Not that I wasn't bored to tears after the excitement of the city.' Clarissa embellished the lie with all the nonchalance of an actress on the stage.

'You missed so much,' Emily sighed, when she recalled the amusements of the past few weeks, drawing forth one or two memories in particular. 'The Penroses' ball was a dreadful squeeze; only think, most of society must have been present.' She laid her head on one side and fluttered her eyelashes. 'Only not Leighton or you, of course. And Annabelle's birthday was a positive romp.'

'Oh, how I should love to have been there,' Clarissa rejoined wistfully, wondering how her vivacious sister could ever have brought herself to miss such fabulous entertainments.

'Don't worry, you'll soon be up to your usual tricks,' Emily prophesied. 'Do you remember the Somerleys' ball?' She laughed and went on to describe exactly the sort of high-jinks Clarissa suspected her sister might get up to.

'I'll be a married woman soon, remember.' Clarissa was sure Marianne would have told the secret of her betrothal to her closest friend, and nor was she disappointed.

'That never stopped you before.'

Clarissa giggled, suddenly warming to her sister's friend. 'No, but it must.' She seized Emily's hand and looked into her eyes. 'I trust to your good sense in keeping my tricks within bounds.'

Emily giggled too. 'You know I have none,' she confided.

Clarissa had already suspected this; Emily was no prattling fool, but her interests clearly ran little further than the latest fashions and enjoying the entertainments offered by society. She herself had other aims, and decided on an attempt to pump the girl. Marianne was still missing, and though her note had indicated she meant to return, a little detective work would surely not go amiss.

'Have you seen Stephen lately?' Clarissa vividly remembered her sister's last communication and the name of the young man she'd mentioned in that letter.

'No.' Emily gripped Clarissa's arm again, her eyes sparkling with excitement. 'I haven't seen him for weeks and nor should you. Leighton is not the man to be teased by a rival.'

'Not for weeks?' Clarissa sounded as disappointed as her friend expected.

'No.' Emily giggled. 'Only think, Meredith was so stupid as to think you had eloped with him.'

'Of course not,' declared Clarissa, wondering just who on earth Meredith was. That was one story she'd have to quash before it developed. 'I shall be officially betrothed to Leighton in a few short weeks, which is just as it should be. One should not forget old friends though.'

'No indeed.' Emily looked serious for once. 'He did you a

great service and he looked so dashing in his regimentals. I only wish he has come to no harm from Dalwinton.'

'Harm?' Clarissa clasped her hands to her bosom. Marianne had written nothing of this.

'I dare say I'm over-reacting. He's more probably returned to his regiment. They're still stationed on the Continent I believe.'

'What about Dalwinton?'

'Leighton will be back in a day or two,' returned Emily easily. 'Dalwinton will back off when he's around, I can tell you. From what I could make out from your aunt, I doubt you'll be out and about much before.'

She drew a book of fashion plates out of her reticule and before long the two were chatting and giggling over the latest fashions just as though they were the two old friends they were supposed to be. Soon they were drawn into discussing the latest and most scandalous of society gossip and news of all their friends, and if Clarissa sometimes displayed an alarming lack of knowledge of events and people she didn't know, Emily seemed neither to notice, nor to care.

CHAPTER FIVE

Lord Leighton

Lord Leighton's morning call sent the Markham household into frenzied preparations. It was Edward who answered his peremptory knock and showed him into the library, before racing down the corridor to apprise Mrs Markham of her unexpected visitor. That lady at once desired her husband to engage his lordship until Clarissa could be made ready, and dispatched Edward to rouse Downing into providing suitable refreshment.

'Sophie too,' she reminded the young footman. 'She must be awaiting Marianne with a change of gown.' The slightest of pauses while she mentally reviewed the girl's wardrobe. 'The sprigged muslin,' she decided, 'and, as for the rest, I will attend Marianne myself.' She couldn't trust the maid, nor Clarissa either, not to make a fashion *faux pas* on this most important of occasions.

'Marianne.' She hurried down a narrow rear corridor, shouting out her niece's *nom de plume* while she headed towards the garden.

'I'm here, Aunt,' said Clarissa, quite unaware that her patient work in arranging fresh blooms in vases was the talk of the servants quarters, since the vivacious Marianne had never concerned herself with anything so mundane. Sophie had been questioned on the matter, though that young lady had stead-fastly refused the chance to make her suspicions public.

'To your room, child, at once,' gasped Eleanor. 'Leighton has returned to Town and seen fit to call upon us. I've desired Sophie lay out the sprigged muslin, which will go very well with the pale-green satin bodice I bought you last month. A chemisette to match the muslin and fill in the neckline also.' Clarissa's aunt knew very well that neither Marianne, nor her maid, would think it out of place to wear a low-cut bodice when attending the man to whom she was secretly betrothed; Clarissa, she judged, had far more good sense, but it was always as well to make sure. 'I'll be up to attend you on the instant.'

Clarissa skipped up the stairs to her room, outwardly showing no trace of the turmoil that troubled her mind. Leighton! She'd counted on him being gone from Town for several more days. Didn't he have enough property to keep him busy? Bad enough she had to nerve herself to fool society; now she had the man her sister was betrothed to on her plate. It was all very well for Aunt Eleanor to insist they'd never been left alone, but she knew Marianne better than her aunt. If her sister had wanted to spend time flirting with the man, she'd have engineered it somehow. Probably have allowed him to kiss her too!

In the event, Clarissa's entry to the library was as triumphant as anything Eleanor could have desired. Her neckline may have been modest, but the classical cut of the flowing muslin drapery clung to her form, emphasizing a neat figure that needed no stays to enhance its slim lines. Gaitered slippers in pale-green kid, matched the pretty half bodice and displayed her delicate feet which twinkled across the floor towards her betrothed.

'Lord Leighton,' she began, then a trifle self-consciously corrected herself. 'Richard. How kind of you to visit when you must be exhausted from all your travelling.' She held out one dainty arm in his direction, silently cursing herself for such a stilted speech.

Leighton, for his part, stood up to receive her, taking her hand languidly in his own and carrying it politely to his lips. It was well done and performed with an ease that told of long practice, but there was a lack of any real emotion in his demeanour that warned Clarissa he wasn't altogether interested in the activities or even the person of his affianced wife. Thank God, was her only coherent thought for this lowering discovery.

'The pleasure is all mine, my love.' Her betrothed made no attempt to hang on to her hand. 'After all the alarming symptoms I'm apprised of, I'm pleased to see you looking so well,' he told her more earnestly than the lazy drawl related. 'It's true I only returned from my estates late last night, but I came at once when I heard the story of how your suffering had forced you to leave Town. I believe you spent some time recuperating at your aunt's house in the country. I should have called upon you there if I'd known.'

Clarissa dropped her head into the slightest of bows. 'I ought to have made it known to you, sir,' she admitted.

'How could you, when you didn't know where I was?' Leighton made little of the affair. 'I should like to know your aunt's direction once we're married, of course, but I hope never to make undue calls on your time.' He bowed and led her to a seat close to his own.

'I fear you wouldn't have been admitted to my bedside even if you had visited, my lord.' Clarissa thanked God Leighton hadn't thought to visit her aunt, though she seriously doubted whether he had any real interest in her imaginary illness. More likely he'd heard the same story Emily had, that Marianne had run off with a penniless officer, and come to discover the truth. At least her appearance would scotch those vicious rumours.

'Your aunt could not have been so unkind as to keep me from you,' he replied to her with a polished, if detached, politeness.

Damn the man, he was acting as off-hand about Marianne's disappearance as … She felt herself blush for her sister. Where was the girl? She was as much to blame as he. The one always playing tricks and him so high in the instep, and for what reason?

Leighton had fallen back into conversation with her uncle with a facility that must have been as galling to Marianne as it was to her. It did, however, give Clarissa the chance to observe him at her leisure without appearing rude.

Richard, Viscount Leighton, stood, she judged, somewhat over six feet in his stockinged feet. Clarissa and her twin, Marianne, were considered quite tall by feminine standards, but he topped her by almost a head, though his height might be somewhat exaggerated by his upright stance which gave him the unfortunate appearance of staring down his nose at one. Late twenties or early thirties, perhaps. A handsome face, she had to admit; a little too long for classical beauty, but regular featured with the most piercingly blue eyes she'd ever seen and a shock of dark, curly hair cut à la Titus. He was fashionably attired in riding dress; a blue superfine jacket moulded to his chest and decorated with gilt buttons over a spotless white shirt with high pointed collar, an elegantly tied cravat à la Trône, tight buckskin pantaloons and immaculately polished hessian boots. The clothes fitted perfectly, but even while he sat at his ease, there was no disguising the strength in his powerful body and muscular thighs.

What a pity, she considered, that he should show such a lack of consideration to the world. Plainly he is full of his own consequence, and for no particular reason. Then more truthfully. No reason! The face and body of an Adonis, riches beyond measure and a title. Does he have a mind? she wondered. Or is this all there is to him?

She frowned when she remembered the stories of his conquests as related by Doctor Pym. He's supposed to have rakish tendencies, she decided, finding it hard to believe it of him. He should appear raffish, she considered, perhaps a bit evil, but he's not; indeed he appeared far more wholesome than anyone with such a reputation had any right to. Then again, his manner: vain, proud, overbearing and conceited even, not the sort of qualities she'd expect many women to be attracted to.

At that moment he turned back towards her and smiled. It was so unexpected she felt as though a hammer had thudded into her chest, and she knew at once why women considered him attractive. No wonder Marianne had been thrilled to find herself betrothed to the man.

'You're very quiet today, Marianne. I hope I didn't catch you unawares.'

'I'm still decidedly groggy from the effects of my illness,' Clarissa admitted, faintly aware that Leighton was turning the full force of his charm on her, and worried he might ferret out the truth of their deception. 'I haven't been out as yet. The party planned by the Rodneys for their daughters will be my first engagement since my return. Have you received an invitation to the event?'

Of course he hadn't, as she knew full well. Thank God the gathering would include a select few only. Going out into society for the first time, especially when she was playing a part was bad enough, but meeting Leighton there would be too much for her nerves to bear. She was to be disappointed.

'I will apply to Rodney immediately,' he assured her. 'We often meet at my club, though we aren't particular friends.'

He's going, she decided, and schooled her face to show pleasure. She had no doubt Rodney would provide the invitation; Leighton, as she'd been told more than once, was the darling of the ton.

'I understand you've taken an interest in the flower garden.' Now where the devil had he learnt that?

'It was ever my passion when I lived with Aunt Constance,' Clarissa was startled into the admission.

'I should never have expected it of you.' His eyebrows had risen in question and Clarissa knew she'd have to keep her wits about her.

'Perhaps there's more in me for you to discover,' she forced herself to simper and giggle nervously, while she played the coquette. It was a role Marianne would have carried off to perfection, but Clarissa was well aware her play hadn't abated his suspicions by one jot.

'Then I will attempt to do just that,' he declared, rising to his feet with all the grace of a hunting panther and holding out one elegant hand. 'Will you show me around the garden now?'

'Oh.' Clarissa found herself on her feet almost before she realized it.

Leighton tucked her arm under his own and bowed to Mr Markham. 'You will permit me, sir?'

'Of course.' Mr Markham had been outflanked and could hardly withhold his permission at this point, not when they were to all intents and purposes betrothed. The garden wasn't so large the couple could truly claim to be alone, but it would provide some opportunity for private speech.

That Leighton had been in the garden before was obvious, and he swiftly led Clarissa down a gravel path that led to a hidden glade amongst the blooming spring flowers. There was a seat waiting there for him to offer her, big enough for the two of them to sit together. Had Marianne attempted a tête-à-tête with him there before she disappeared?

She sat down carefully, seating herself towards one end of the bench to allow him the space to do likewise. Then she eyed him intently, concerned in case he should attempt to kiss her. Anxious too, Marianne might have allowed him that freedom in the past.

'Tell me, child,' he began, 'were you really at your aunt's?'

'Yes. Where else would I have gone?' It was, of course, the plain, unvarnished truth so far as her own movements were concerned, and Clarissa, who was prescient enough to see he believed her, felt a moment of shame in deceiving him. Damn Marianne, what was she playing at?

'I can only apologize for bringing such suspicions to your notice. You must forgive me for giving any credence to rumours about your disappearance.' Leighton showed a rare moment of concern for the girl. 'Society feeds on the most ugly gossip.'

So he had heard the same stories as Emily, Clarissa decided. 'Her gardens are particularly lovely at this time of year,' she went on, prattling in a vain attempt to cover up her momentary lapse from character.

'You have changed.'

For a moment Clarissa panicked, but there was a curious half smile on his lips, and she suddenly realized his words hadn't constituted an accusation, more a prompt for her to follow.

'I have?' she quavered.

'Perhaps not,' he laughed harshly. 'More likely it is I. We hardly had the chance to get to know each other in the constant round of entertainments.' He went oddly quiet. 'I should like to do that now, if you please?' His eyebrows once again rose in a way that Clarissa found curiously endearing.

'Perhaps we can speak further at Colonel Rodney's,' she corroborated. 'I dare swear you will obtain that invitation.'

Clarissa knew she was being deliberately coquettish and attempted to excuse herself on account of the role she had to play, but that was a lie that brought her no relief. She knew the truth; knew that Leighton affected her, just as his own interest had been piqued, and berated herself for seeking what her sister already had. Where was the girl?

'I thought I might plan an expedition too, a picnic by the river.' He spoke lazily, as though visualizing the scene in his mind's eye. 'With your aunt's permission, of course. My sister and her husband will accompany us, and you may invite your friend Emily as well. I dare say some others might also be counted on.'

'How lovely.' Well, and so it was, she decided, still quite unable to decide whether she was accepting for herself or the role she was playing. The answer to that question came easily enough when she wondered whether Marianne would have returned by the time that particular project got under way, and realized how disappointed she'd be to miss the trip.

Leighton didn't seem to notice her distraction, and they were soon deep in conversation, allowing him to draw some interesting confidences from her. On her own part, Clarissa realized she'd have to rethink some of her scorn for him; there was a light of intelligence in his eyes, no little knowledge and a quiet sense of humour. Not at all what she'd expected.

Later, up in her room dressing for dinner, she sought to address her feelings. That his interest had been piqued, she already knew. By her, or by Marianne? He'd made it plain his affections hadn't previously been drawn, but in all probability Marianne would have done the same once she had him to herself. Clarissa knew just how taking her sister could be when she chose to amuse.

Did he share the same little intimacies with Marianne as he'd shared with her? She felt a jolt of disappointment; he must, it was only her foolishness that made it seem she was special. It was Marianne he loved, not her dowdy sister, Clarissa. It was Marianne he was betrothed to.

The violence of her feelings chafed on her nerves, and caused her to throw caution to the winds. Sophie was dressing her hair and she attempted to question her maid, determined to make some headway in tracking down her sister before her own heart was drawn any further into danger.

'Sophie.'

'Yes, ma'am.'

Clarissa hesitated, finding once more how hard it was to ask for clues to her own whereabouts.

'Did I ever speak to you about Stephen?' She instinctively felt the shadowy figure of Stephen figured in the mystery of Marianne's disappearance.

'Stephen, ma'am?' The maid's answering tone was blank. Deliberately so, Clarissa decided.

'Of no matter. Emily told me he's rejoined his regiment anyway.' She looked up at Sophie's expression, but it was schooled into the same indifference it always held. Clarissa decided, not for the first time, that she'd given something away the first day they'd met.

'I expect so, ma'am.'

It was too bad of the girl. Did she know something of Marianne's disappearance? They'd been thick as thieves, or so

Aunt Eleanor believed. She cursed inwardly, realizing she could never ask the direct questions she'd like to without giving the game away completely.

CHAPTER SIX

A Select Assembly

Clarissa wouldn't have been human if she hadn't been excited by the thought of her first London party, but there was a touch of anxiety too, when she sat in her petticoats, nervously adjusting the tilt of her head while Sophie dressed her hair. It was evening, time to prepare for the night ahead, and though she'd often attended private parties and assemblies in her own locality, she knew that none of these could come close to the magnificence of the event she'd been promised by her aunt. Her enthusiastic description of the lavish refreshments and entertainments likely to be on offer, seemed to deny rather than enhance the supposed exclusivity of the event.

Sophie, too, seemed a different girl, much more particular in her attentions and laughing with her mistress in exactly the manner Clarissa had expected of a maidservant who'd been her sister's confidante, while she exclaimed gleefully over the beautiful dress her charge was to wear for the first time that evening. Aunt Eleanor had bought the article for Marianne only a day or two before that young woman had disappeared and she hadn't even had the chance to display it to her friends.

Not that Clarissa's excitement over her first London

engagement was wholly unalloyed; she'd have to meet and greet a multitude of people who knew Marianne well, and although her aunt had undertaken to remain at her side throughout the evening, the girl was well aware that might prove impossible. Of course, she already had a friend in Emily, and Lord Leighton, too. Surely if those two accepted her as Marianne, then it would take a bold individual to cavil at the suggestion she was her sister. The girl shook her head ruefully and allowed she was close to confusing herself with her identity, let alone anyone else.

Her chosen raiment was not quite to her liking. Marianne, she knew, was by far the more vivacious of the pair of them, and while most certainly not fast, easily drawn into wearing more daring fashions. Like her sister who'd chosen it, Clarissa was overwhelmed by the simple beauty of the dress, and, of course, she could hardly refuse to wear such an expensive gift from her patroness. Nevertheless she had to admit to qualms about its neckline, which, to her mind, was cut too low for a girl in her first season. When consulted, Aunt Eleanor had laughingly dismissed her fears as quite ridiculous when Marianne was well known to be close to an engagement with Leighton, and added an alarming rider that her sister had complained it was by far too modest.

Too late for recriminations though, when her maid was drawing her to her feet and turning her around to judge the effect she'd achieved.

'La, you're so pretty, miss. Lord Leighton is like to be jealous of the attention you'll receive.' Her lovely little face was lit up with such joy for her mistress that Clarissa could easily forget her suspicions that the girl might have realized she was a changeling.

At last she was dressed and ready for the off. A pale sarsnet petticoat, full flounce around the hem; high plain body of white jaconard muslin with long full sleeve, confined at the wrist and trimmed with lace, adorned with the most exquisite and skilfully wrought white embroidery; ribbed stockings to match, with lace clocks that might be seen in the swirl of the dance; last of all the matching shoes of pale queen silk. Even Clarissa gave a gasp when she finally got to see herself in the mirror and had to admit that the low square neckline, though more revealing than she'd ever choose herself, suited the garment perfectly.

'Shall I damp your petticoats, miss?'

The maid's question gave Clarissa pause. She was playing a part for her sister, and had to consider if, after several weeks of London society and the inevitable sophistication it gave, Marianne would have resorted to such scandalous tricks as damping her petticoats the better to display her figure.

'No, thank you, Sophie.' Of course, Marianne would have refused such a request. She had too much good sense, and besides, her figure was graceful enough without any such enhancement to draw attention to it. Clarissa blushed, realizing she was complimenting herself also, for in form as well as face, they were completely alike. In any case Leighton would be there. Clarissa had no intention of drawing his eye any more than was necessary, and neither did she think he would approve of such tricks, though when she advanced this reasoning to her maid, the girl returned a saucy answer.

'He wouldn't mind, miss. Not if half I've heard about him is true. Why, Lady Darcross is said to do it all the time.'

'Lady Darcross?' From all Clarissa had learned of Lady Darcross, despite being in Town for little more than a week, damping her petticoats was the least of her sins. Though what that lady had to do with her was too much to imagine, and following her immediate exclamation, she confined herself to the question of Lord Leighton. 'He would not expect to find such behaviour in his betrothed, Sophie,' she declared.

'Yes, miss,' agreed the maid, in an immediate *volte face*. 'I expect you're right.' Then she went on to complain so bitterly that Clarissa wondered if she'd fallen into the same trap herself. 'All the gentlemen are the same, young or old. It don't matter what a cake they make of themselves, just so long as you don't try to deal with them in the same coin.'

She wondered, too, at the change in her maid. Perhaps she'd been won over at last, and had forgotten any suspicions she might have had. Indeed, she could have found no proof, of that much Clarissa was certain. With some encouragement, Sophie might be persuaded to open up. If Marianne had left of her own free will, and that seemed likely from all the clues they'd turned up so far, then someone must have seen her go. Perhaps the maid had packed for her, was even in her confidence, or if not, then at least could have noticed clothing missing. Marianne, whatever her reasons for vacating the Markhams' house, would never have left herself with an insufficient wardrobe.

There was no time this evening, the party was almost upon her, but perhaps she could quiz the girl later.

The Rodneys' party delighted Clarissa. Despite the exclusivity of its company, to an inexperienced girl it appeared to be all that a full-blown ball should be. If the crushed ranks of society attending didn't constitute a squeeze, then how many guests would have to be invited to accomplish such a feat?

Out on the wide square that fronted the Rodneys' mansion, liveried staff were busily attempting to make some sort of order amongst the serried ranks of carriages from which the guests descended on their hosts. Such lively imbroglios amongst the drivers and footmen jockeying for position were diverting enough in themselves, but when at last she and Aunt Eleanor descended to join the constant throng queuing into the house, Clarissa was able to admire at length the wonderfully attired gentry awaiting entry. She was also aware, and not entirely immune from, the admiring glances sent her own way. Many, also, appeared to recognize her, waving and nodding in a way that she instantly made an attempt to emulate.

'Keep close,' she warned her aunt. 'Everyone seems to know me.' Or know Marianne, she corrected herself silently, suddenly realizing how exposed she was in her role.

In the event, she and her aunt were separated the moment they'd passed the line. Colonel Rodney was a tall, bluff man, who looked every inch the regimental commander: a tall, thickset man with a bluff, honest manner whom Clarissa thought quite charming. His wife was just as open, and paid Clarissa a very generous compliment on her appearance, especially since it was her own daughters she would naturally want to shine.

'My dear,' she went on, 'you have such pretty manners too. Just the sort of girl I would wish Fanny to take up with.'

Fanny turned out to be her eldest, next in line and painfully shy at her first attempt as a hostess. Clarissa already knew she was due to be presented within a month or two, Emily's gossip had seen to that. But despite her friend's reservations, Clarissa couldn't see anything dowdy in either Fanny or her mother. Both were beautifully turned out, and though their gowns might be termed modest, they didn't in the least lack style.

Clarissa had already spotted Emily with a group of other girls of a similar age trying to catch her attention. They were evidently Marianne's special cronies and no good would come of any attempt to avoid them. Nor could she even think of it when she was playing the vivacious role her sister would have been the first to applaud.

'Please feel free to join us once your duties here are finished,' she offered, smiling brightly at Fanny, who blushed and thanked her with a profusion that spoke volumes of her nervousness.

Jane was the younger sister, though she was nearly as tall as her sibling, and more voluble. Plainly she didn't suffer from her elder sister's shyness. Not that she didn't have her own charm, excited by the occasion no doubt, but too well mannered to be thought of as pert.

'Only guess, Marianne.' Emily took hold of Clarissa's arm as soon as she could, and led her off into the midst of a chattering crowd of young misses, around which a gaggle of eligible young men was already gathering to press their claims for the dances ahead. 'Chatsbury tells me Leighton has been busy engaging a yacht for our expedition on the river.'

Clarissa could only guess who Chatsbury was, but took note of the name. If he knew of Leighton's plans then he was presumably a particular crony of the viscount and it would be as well to know of his existence.

'That's wonderful,' she replied warmly, if a trifle vacantly. Well, it was wonderful, she told herself, and she would be excited when the time came. A yacht on the river! But she couldn't even think of the future when the present was so perilously close.

With Marianne's friends around her, her heart was in her throat for fear of exposing her role, though she soon found those fears groundless. She'd heard enough society gossip from Emily to join in light-hearted discussions on the latest news, and since that and the prevailing fashions were the chief subjects of conversation, she had no doubt of her ability to carry through her deception. She was soon in command of all their names and, in addition, most of the passers-by also, from the greetings to which she listened with an ardent dedication. Her card was rapidly filling as well, and she was soon aware of just how much in vogue her sister had been. Every young person in the room seemed to make it his or her business to speak to her.

Fanny joined them when her duties as hostess allowed, and Clarissa reintroduced the girls to her, adding a short monologue on each, with only one mistake.

'Marianne,' cried out one young maiden, 'you know I'm first cousin to Fanny and my father was in Colonel Rodney's regiment forever. We've played together since she was out of leading strings.'

'I didn't like to miss you out,' Clarissa returned unblushingly. 'I dare say several of you know Fanny and she you, but this is her first dance as an adult and it's important to be a success. I remember my first ball. A proper fool I felt, knowing no one, and wondering how to behave. I swear I should have run off if I could have found the door through the crowd.'

'Not you,' Emily laughed, and threw her arm around Clarissa's waist. 'You would only have run off with the most handsome man in the room.' She broke off and stared at the figure fast approaching the mirthful group.

'Leighton,' Clarissa breathed the word through lips that barely opened. She was suddenly aware that her heart was hammering and an idiot smile was forming on her face.

'Marianne.' He ignored the throng around her, scattering them like chaff in the wind, while he took charge of her hand and raised it to his lips.

'Richard.' She tried to play down the pleasure rippling through her, ashamed of her behaviour in greeting her sister's future husband with such fervour, but she just couldn't stop herself reacting to his presence. I have to appear complaisant for the sake of my role, she tried to convince herself, but she knew that reasoning was pure humbug. She liked this man too much.

'I hope you've saved a dance for me?'

'Oh, yes.' Clarissa saved her blushes by staring intently at the card in her hands. 'One only,' she offered shyly.

'Then I'll take it,' he murmured, slipping one finger under her chin to tip up her face, 'and this one also.'

Dimly Clarissa was aware that a set was forming and a gangly youth was attempting to claim her attention.

'Oh no, I'm afraid—'

Leighton had all the address of a man who'd been on the Town for years on his side. 'My dear boy,' he began, 'I'm so sorry to cut you out, but I'm sure you'll understand. Marianne and I have been parted for so long and have much to discuss before our betrothal.'

The lad was left with nothing to do but bow politely towards the pair.

'Richard,' Clarissa blushingly told off her partner while they made their way to the dance floor. 'You are the most unprincipled of men.'

'I know,' he admitted, but failed to show any significant remorse for his actions, merely twirling her on to the floor for the start of the first country dance.

'Are you going to serve all my partners so badly?' she managed to get out before the music started.

'No,' he admitted, once the steps of the dance permitted. 'I already have another dance secured, and until we are formally betrothed it would be lacking in delicacy to take you to the floor more than twice in a night.' The dance separated them for a moment more. 'You would no doubt be categorized as fast at once,' he went on with a smile that lanced through her heart when they came together again. 'I shall, however, expect you to favour me with your presence once the refreshments are available.'

Clarissa nodded her head in agreement. 'No doubt Emily will lend us countenance,' she teased, thankful that in deference to Fanny and Jane's youth, the waltz was not to be played that evening. She was in a flutter enough without being twirled around the floor in his arms!

Lord Leighton was not a man to be denied, however. When the time came to convey refreshments to his lady, he made sure that Emily was diverted elsewhere, cutting out Clarissa from her friends with a grace and charm that made her blush.

Aunt Eleanor caught sight of the pair by the doors that led into the garden, and attempted to intercept them, but the young viscount was too quick for her.

'The colonel tells me his orangery is the envy of all London,' he told Clarissa, luring her over the threshold and into the ornamental garden. 'I believe we'll find it through the rose arch.'

Clarissa raised her eyes and thought of refusing, but there was a sparkle in his that gave her pause. Damn you, Marianne, she complained silently. I'm doing this for you. And blushed for her lies, because at a baser level she knew she'd follow him anywhere. Seeing her hesitation, Leighton raised his glass in salute and pointed out the way with a mocking smile lighting up his face.

'You are a connoisseur of orangeries, sir?' Clarissa fought back, knowing very well he'd spotted her indecision. But not, she considered, with a knowing smile of her own, the reasons for her reluctance.

'There are succession houses at several of my properties,' he said, tempering his interest, and tucking her hand neatly under his arm. 'I dare say there is something of the sort at my London house, too, though I cannot claim an intimate knowledge of it.'

'Then the rose garden may be a better place to start, my lord.' She waved her hand around to indicate they were already there, but deliberately denied herself the use of his given name. That would have been too dangerous for her already wavering sensibilities. 'We are quite alone here.' She smiled up at him bewitchingly. 'I assume you wish to speak with me in private and I must soon return or risk being thought less than virtuous.'

The look Leighton graced her with told Clarissa that he did indeed want to get her alone. For more than speech too, if she were any judge. Not that such a young, inexperienced girl as she was any judge, though she was seasoned enough to see he had to master his feelings before he spoke.

'You must forgive me for being so unlover-like in the past, my dear,' he began. 'I beg your indulgence, but I am here to change all that. I cannot think why I never paid you much attention before.'

'Perhaps you were too busy with Lady Darcross.' Clarissa drew a bow at random and saw she'd scored a direct hit. 'Oh,' she gasped, utterly distraught. 'Is she one of your flirts?'

'She is in the past.' Leighton's angry scowl suddenly gave way to a careless laugh. 'Lady Darcross is not a suitable subject for conversation between us, nor should anyone have been foolish enough to tell you about my amours.'

'I'm sorry,' she admitted. 'I didn't really know ...' Her voice fell away while she nerved herself to ask the question. 'Only – was she very beautiful?' And cursed herself for evading what she really wanted to know.

'She was, indeed still is,' he replied, 'but, as I told you, that particular lady is in the long dead past.'

'You loved her?'

'I thought so once, but only for a while.'

'Do you have many amours?'

'Enough,' he replied, strangely disconcerted by Clarissa's candour. 'Let us talk instead about the future.'

'The future?'

'You, chit, belong to the future.' He grasped her shoulders, turning her to face him.

'Oh.' Her lips parted slightly when his smouldering glance scorched through her, and the unexpected sensations searing through her body surprised a gasp from her lips.

'You have bewitched me, Marianne.' His hands tightened their hold and Clarissa had the odd feeling he was going to sweep her off her feet and into his arms. Her lips opened of their own accord to accept his sweet kisses, and then the import of what he'd said hit her. Marianne, this was all for Marianne.

The honeyed words he was whispering in her ears, the intimacies he was suggesting. These should all have been shared with her sister. Not her. Not Clarissa. And she was the guilty one. She wanted those sweet words for herself. God alone knew, she wanted him to kiss her. Wanted him to kiss Clarissa. Wanted it with all her heart, and all her being.

'No,' she cried distractedly, and tore herself out of his arms.

'My apologies.' Leighton clenched his hands into tight fists, mastering himself as well as he could. God, but the chit had all but scattered his wits. 'I frightened you,' he continued, his natural concern coming to the fore. 'I should have taken my fences more easily.'

'No.' Clarissa laid a comforting hand on his arm. 'It was not you who lost their head, but me.'

'Then you do not find me unacceptable?'

'Of course not, Richard.' The girl allowed herself the comfort of using his name. Pray God Marianne returned before she had to again.

'Thank God.' He uttered the words out loud, totally unabashed by Clarissa's wide-eyed stare.

'Tell me how you obtained an invitation?' She brought the subject back to the prosaic while they began to stroll back towards the ballroom. 'I heard the gathering was very select.'

'Am I not select?'

'You are insufferable, sir.' Clarissa tapped his hand with her own, 'and have a care, for we are no longer alone.' She stared up at him with a wistful look that struck him to the core.

'Colonel Rodney is always glad to entertain an old campaigner,' he told her. 'I never had the honour of serving in his regiment, but I saw him often when I was attached to Wellington's staff.'

'You were a soldier?'

'Why so surprised, chit? Many young men were.'

'You were the heir. The viscount.'

'Not until my brother died of the influenza.' A sad, far away look entered his eyes, and he laughed harshly. 'I was fighting in the Peninsula, facing death on a daily basis and yet it was he who suffered and died.' He recovered his poise and admitted his feelings. 'D'Arcy and I were very close; no more than ten months apart. Funnily enough, it was always I who was the delicate one. He never endured a day's sickness in his life, until the epidemic hit our estates.' He shook off his mournful expression. 'My father died soon after and I succeeded. I had to sell out then.'

'Sophie.'

'Yes, miss?' The maid's new found air of devotion continued into the early hours of the morning when she helped Clarissa out of her clothes.

'My check shawl. You know the one, with a slight tear in one corner. Have you seen it lately?' Clarissa hadn't seen the article since she'd arrived at the Markhams' house, and Marianne had always valued it for its warmth despite its forlorn appearance.

'You gave it to me, miss.' Sophie turned a surprised look on her mistress. 'For my sister, the last time I took a half day.'

Clarissa immediately begged pardon, but she'd detected the slightest of pauses before the girl answered. Sophie was a good little actress, but Clarissa decided she knew more than she was letting on about Marianne's disappearance. What's more, the question, though designed to catch out the maid, must also have proved to Sophie she was dealing with a changeling in her mistress. Did she know Marianne had a twin?

'I've another due, miss.'

'Another?' Clarissa turned questioning eyes on her maid.

'Half day, miss. Later on in the week, if that's all right with you.'

'Oh yes, of course. Will you visit your family again?'

'Sure to, miss.'

CHAPTER SEVEN

---⚬⚬⚬---

A Pleasure Trip

The sailing barge was taken up at Westminster, to which part of town the ladies in the party had been conveyed by an open carriage. Amongst the women, and in addition to Clarissa, Leighton had invited her friend Emily, and at Clarissa's special request, young Fanny Rodney. Lady Burnett, Leighton's sister, with whom Clarissa was not yet acquainted, made up the party in the barouche, jokingly referring to herself as being there to maintain the proprieties. When it became apparent that Marianne was already on good terms with the lady, Clarissa was inclined to view her inclusion as unfortunate, but she soon found Caroline, as she begged them all to call her, a particularly agreeable young lady with whom she was quickly seen to be fast friends.

Leighton's particular companion, Lord Chatsbury, rode with him alongside the carriage, while a few yards behind, Sir Roger Burnett, his brother-in-law and Caroline's husband, was deep in conversation with young Roderick Thornton, invited to make up the numbers as a sop to being so ruthlessly cut out of Clarissa's dance card at the Rodneys'. Since he'd known Fanny since she was in short coats and the pair of them dealt together well, Clarissa decided Leighton had made an extremely good choice.

The picnic had been bespoke along with the sailing barge, so there was no more to do than board the boat themselves before it cast off and began to tack upriver. They were aiming for Richmond, but at this state of the tide it was a slow journey, and the party soon settled down with some refreshments served by a good-natured young woman who was evidently a regular part of the crew.

Clarissa was particularly pleased to find that Caroline took her duties seriously and forbade Fanny the wine that was offered, though with such good-natured banter the girl couldn't take her interference as anything but the best advice. Clarissa, too, was more than happy to drink a refreshing draught of lemonade, freshly cooled over the side of the vessel.

At first she engaged herself in desultory conversation with Caroline, Emily and Fanny, but, all too soon, Leighton himself came to stand by her side. The other women naturally drew back and left the pair to themselves, where he contented himself in tarrying with her.

'Richard,' Chatsbury called out to his friend, from his position in the bows where he was standing with the other men. 'Are you to be forever tied to your wife's apron strings?'

Leighton replied by holding up his wine glass in an ironic salute and bowing towards them.

'Come, man, you're not even married as yet,' Chatsbury continued ribbing his friend.

The three men laughed out loud at this sally, but Leighton wasn't in the least discomforted by their amusement.

'Marianne's company,' he told them good-naturedly, 'is infinitely to be preferred to your own coarse manners.'

'You needn't stay just to keep me company,' Clarissa told him quietly, but he only grinned at her, looking so boyish that she felt the strangest urge to run her fingers through his hair.

'I can assure you, my dear, it's not duty that makes me stay at your side, but rather that I want to. Your conversation and wit is proving more refreshing than I ever thought possible.' Then, more drily, 'Perhaps I should have got to know you better earlier in our acquaintanceship.'

'Perhaps, my lord.'

'Richard.' His hand closed over hers on the rail when he corrected her, and she felt the warmth run up her arm.

'Richard,' she repeated, her lips trembling on the name, 'but you will put me to the blush if you continue to hold my hand so noticeably.'

'Then you must blush, my dear.'

Leighton was as good as his word in that he stayed at her side throughout the slow progress upriver, lazily making conversation, though, to her infinite relief, he released her hand at length.

The picnic was taken on the bank a short distance below Richmond itself. A wide expanse of greensward provided enough space to set out the repast and several well trodden paths led into the lightly wooded common grounds about its perimeter.

'I never saw you in such grig,' Emily twitted her, while they ate together on an old shawl the serving woman laid out for them, 'and you're getting on wonderfully well with Leighton.'

Clarissa had been aware of just how often she'd been brought to the point of laughter by her skilful admirer, but she had hoped it wouldn't be as obvious to her companions. She blushed and answered with unexpected brevity. 'Yes, I am, aren't I?'

'You were such a goose to wonder about him, Marianne, and moon over another after he'd offered.'

'Another? And who would that be?' Clarissa instinctively realized that here was a clue to Marianne's disappearance if only she could extract any meaning from it.

'La!' Emily playfully slapped Clarissa's wrist with her fan. 'You're so inconstant.' Then she fixed her eyes on Leighton with an assessing, even predatory, stare. 'I should not play fast and loose with such a man if I were in your position.'

'Neither do I mean to.' Clarissa blushed to the roots of her hair when she made the statement. Of course she meant to; however often she should meet the man, it was her sister who would have him, and suddenly she realized just what that meant to her. 'I don't!' she declared so plainly, that Leighton's sister, seated a short distance hence, turned towards her in surprise.

'Come sit with me,' she invited. Sir Roger, who'd been relaxing at his ease by her side, instantly leapt to his feet and offered his place.

'I've been meaning to get better acquainted with your friend,' he told her politely, 'if young Chatsbury doesn't cut me out first.'

Clarissa smiled and thanked him. 'No one could be so distinguished as to cut you out, sir,' she assured him, while she swapped places to talk to Caroline.

'I'm intrigued,' that lady began enigmatically. 'I have to admit that when I first heard of the match between you, I was worried Richard might have mistaken himself. He succeeded unexpectedly when our brother died childless and realized he must marry for the sake of the succession; indeed the family were adamant on the matter. He would have wanted a love match for himself, I'm sure, but I was persuaded his offer was made only because your beauty and wit were the toast of the town. As the last of the Leighton line, I was convinced he thought he owed it to his position to choose only such a nonpareil as his partner. I see now I was wrong, and that it is truly a love match.'

Clarissa found herself put to the blush again. The knowledge she was deceiving not only the man she loved, but also so many other good people, worried her desperately. The man she loved! Oh my God, she blushed to the roots of her hair when she realized it was so; that she'd known it all along, ever since the first moment they'd met. She was in love with the one man in the world she couldn't have. Richard belonged to her sister, though by some strange additional sense that fluttered deep in her breast, she also realized that it was her, Clarissa, that Leighton was wooing. For once, her more vivacious sister, Marianne, was having to take second place.

Perhaps she could reveal the truth? Her heart hung heavy when she considered the option. She could never find it in her heart to cut out her own dear sister, and neither would it answer if she could. If the truth were known then such a scandal would arise as would shame her and Marianne forever. Leighton, and all his family too, would hate such notoriety, and she dreaded seeing the dawning look of horror on his face when he realized how they'd fooled him and made him the butt of every joker in society.

'I'm sorry.' Caroline laid a calming hand on Clarissa's arm, concerned by the emotions she saw reflected in the girl's face. 'I have over-set you with my well-meaning tittle tattle.'

'No.' Clarissa cleared her conscience with an effort. 'You are right. It is a love match; for me, at least.' She was playing a part, but that much was true, she reflected ruefully.

'I don't think you have any need to doubt Richard's feelings,' Caroline replied. 'I've never seen him so desperately in love.'

'You're too kind, ma'am.' Clarissa resorted to a formality she scarcely felt to relieve her feelings.

'My friends call me Caro,' Leighton's sister replied, 'and I'm sure we're going to be the greatest of friends.'

'I do hope so,' – there was the smallest of pauses – 'Caro.' Clarissa was once again in part. Marianne's standing in society was at stake and she couldn't play traitor to her sister however much her own peace of mind might be put at risk.

'Are you fully recovered from your illness?' Caroline turned the conversation to less dangerous subjects, despite her own natural inquisitiveness. She'd realized instinctively that Clarissa was hiding something, a secret that might affect her brother's future happiness, but she couldn't see what it could possibly be. She'd swear on her life the girl was in love with him, and he with her. Then what could be the trouble?

Following the repast, the gentlemen teamed up with the ladies while they strolled about the common, and Clarissa soon found herself paired off with Leighton and deep in conversation. Somehow they'd wandered far enough along the river-bank to find themselves alone. At first the girl had wondered at the wisdom of such a move, but soon resolved she'd play her part. She might not have Leighton's companionship for long, and it was up to her to take what comfort from it she could while she was still able.

'Tell me about your life,' she begged, anxious to store up such memories as she could.

'What do you want to know?' he laughed.

'I already know you soldiered in the Peninsula,' she declared. 'You were on Wellington's staff. Did you know the Duke himself?'

'I had that honour, though I dare say he barely noticed me,'

Leighton returned modestly. 'I was only a young officer largely used to carry his dispatches to the regiments under his command.'

'That sounds dangerous.' Clarissa couldn't stop herself from clutching apprehensively at his arm.

'Not especially. In my position I was rarely to be found in the forefront of the action.'

'Colonel Rodney has a high opinion of you,' she charged.

'Overrated, I'm sad to say.' He stared down at Clarissa's flushed face, feeling the rising passion in his own breast, and made the confession. 'I fought with him once. Having delivered my dispatches I found myself trapped and the regimental head-quarters surrounded. It was a desperate battle for a while, until reinforcements came upon us.'

'Were you happy to sell out?' Clarissa decided she didn't want to hear about the danger he'd been in any more.

'Not at the time,' he temporized. 'I loved life as an officer in the Peninsula. We weren't under fire all the time and I made some real friendships. Succession to the title changed all that: I had to sell out, the family demanded it, indeed my position demanded it. Yet I found society strangely dull and restricted after the freedom of life in the army. In addition I missed the final assault on the French positions, on France itself.'

'You were bored?'

'I suppose that was the case,' he admitted. 'I had plenty to amuse me, but somehow the delights of society never proved enough. I was the head of the family, the noble Viscount Leighton, but all my heartfelt ambitions seemed to have been taken away from me. I began to game ever more deeply, but win or lose, it was all the same to me.' He looked down at her, almost sheepishly. 'Even Lady Darcross, experienced as she was, couldn't totally banish the ennui.' He paused before admitting a confession that thrilled her. 'I thought I could never be truly happy again, until I got to know you.'

'Yet you managed to tear yourself away for several weeks while you toured your estates,' Clarissa accused him. Then backed off, startled by the light of passion in his eyes.

'It wasn't until I returned I realized how sorely I missed you, how much my heart had changed,' he murmured and snaking out one long, muscular arm, caught her around the waist.

Clarissa finally realized just how charged the air between them had become and made an abortive, and not altogether convincing, attempt to break free. He was going to kiss her, she was perfectly sure of it this time. Would Marianne have allowed such a liberty? She couldn't think so, even though the girl hadn't been above such missish tricks in their youth.

She realized he was lowering his head, his eyes open, searching for the passion in her own. She couldn't stop him, didn't wish to stop him; was no longer acting a part for the sake of her sister, but giving in to her own foolish feelings. The heady realization of love mixed freely with the swirling desire in her brain, and turned it to mush.

The kiss was meant to have been no more than a polite salute, but it drove Clarissa's feelings into the open. She responded with a fervency that she, let alone he, could hardly have expected of herself, twining her arms around his broad shoulders, sliding her fingers through the thicker hair at his nape and parting her lips to taste the renewed passion of his own.

He knew this was madness, to kiss the girl so passionately out in the open, no more than a few hundred yards from their friends. To kiss the girl at all! But he too was caught in the web of desire, and so he drew her closer, glorying in the way her supple curves fitted so close against his own hard body. His lips bore down harder and he crushed her lithe form against him.

Even in the midst of such heartfelt passion, Clarissa's heart missed a beat. She'd begun to suspect, but now she knew it for the truth. It was Clarissa he loved, not Marianne! However briefly, she'd reached the heights of paradise, before reality returned with a rush. As it did!

With a cry of horror, she broke away from his embrace. She'd given in to passion and her own selfish desires. She'd betrayed her sister! She turned and ran.

'Marianne.' Caroline Burnett caught the girl as she rushed towards the barge. 'My dear, you're crying.'

'No.' Clarissa tried to deny it, but to her dismay she tasted the salty tang where one wet tear slid down her cheek and ended up in the corner of her mouth. 'Please,' she whispered, 'no one must know.'

'So it was Richard,' his sister declared. 'He couldn't wait. Just like all the other gentlemen! They never can, my dear,' and she held her young friend close, stroking her hair and calming her nerves.

'No, it wasn't his fault,' Clarissa admitted, facing up to what she'd done. 'He must never realize.' Oh God, if Leighton should ever realize?

'Never realize?' Caroline fought to reconcile the words with the weeping girl in her arms. 'Do you mean to tell me you responded?'

'I shouldn't have.' Clarissa sank her head deeper into the comfort of her new friend's bosom.

'Of course you should,' Caroline laughed. Then she coloured swiftly. 'Well, perhaps not prior to your betrothal, but I can assure you that once you're safely married, you'll be happy to respond to all his advances.'

'You're very kind.' Clarissa stood tall and began to dry her eyes. She had a role to perform and she intended to continue playing it. Richard had captured her heart, but she knew she could never show it so passionately again. He belonged to Marianne, and she straight away resolved the role wouldn't be allowed to last much longer, both for his sake, and for her own.

Leighton eventually caught her alone while their friends were embarking on the sailing barge for the journey back to Westminster.

'I must apologize for my behaviour,' he began stiffly, with the oddest feeling he'd bungled the entire affair.

'No need, Richard.' Clarissa turned calm eyes on his own. 'Your kisses were no more than I wanted from you.' The truth was reflected in those vivid green orbs, and the viscount breathed a sigh of relief.

CHAPTER EIGHT

Clarissa Turns Detective

Next morning Clarissa woke early, determined to dedicate herself to the search for her sister. Not only was her own heart in danger, but the date for Marianne's formal betrothal to Lord Leighton was looming ever closer. Leighton, too, was increasingly becoming a factor in the arrangement. What with her undisguised preference for him, if they continued to meet he would surely spot the change when Marianne reappeared.

'Aunt Eleanor.' Clarissa began the interrogation once break-fast was over and the two of them were left alone. 'We must speak further about Marianne's disappearance. Do you have the note she left?'

'In my writing desk, but you've already seen it once.' Eleanor's voice quavered. In all truth she'd hoped to see Clarissa content to continue the deception, but it was clear that for whatever reason the girl was even more determined to pursue her sister's disappearance.

'I'd like to look at it again, if you don't mind?'

'Well, no, of course not.' No good would come of going after the girl, in her aunt's opinion. Clearly the silly chit had left of her own accord, leaving them to clean up the mess she'd left behind, just as her mother had done all those years before. Nevertheless she could see just how worried Clarissa was for her sister and, despite quaking in her slippers when she thought of the possible repercussions, she led the girl into her private sitting-room.

Clarissa had, of course, been in the room on previous occasions, but never seen the elegant writing desk opened. Eleanor removed a key from the top drawer and deftly opened a secret compartment hidden in its depths. She removed a somewhat soiled and dog-eared wafer, and handed it to her niece.

'It came in this envelope?' Clarissa turned a puzzled eye on her aunt. 'I saw only the note itself before.'

'That is what Sophie handed to us on the morning she left. Is there anything wrong with it?'

'How did it get so dirty?' the girl continued to question her aunt.

'Perhaps … oh, I don't know.' Eleanor threw up her arms in despair. 'Does it matter?'

'I believe so, Aunt.' Clarissa stared at the wafer in her hand. 'It's like no other I've seen in the house. There are envelopes in Marianne's – my room. It's quite unlike those, and yet you would have expected her to have written the missive there, where she'd find privacy. Will I find any envelopes like this in Mr Markham's study?' She held it up.

'No.' Aunt Eleanor found herself struck by the same thought that bothered her niece. 'The quality is very poor. Perhaps there are some like that in the servants' quarters.'

'Perhaps, but I don't suppose Marianne would have fetched them, and neither would the envelope be so dog-eared if Sophie did so for her.'

'What do you mean? It was in that condition when Sophie delivered it to us. If Marianne wrote it here, then, depend on it, she had the wafer from one of the servants.'

'Having seen the state of this wafer, I'm inclined to believe that Marianne wrote the note elsewhere. Somewhere she didn't command the use of quality stationery.' Clarissa opened the wafer and drew out the note. The paper was cheap, but it was at least clean, though it didn't match the envelope it had been taken from. 'She would need to have it delivered in that case. Did any of your servants mention a note being delivered to Sophie?'

'No, though I don't suppose they'd have told me if they did. The mistress of the house can have little interest in her servants' correspondence. Particularly a maidservant of her age.'

'They would remember if she did, however. Sophie is not likely to receive such notes very often.'

'I'll ring for Downing. He can institute enquiries.'

'I think not, Aunt.' Clarissa held up a warning hand to stop her carrying out such an action. 'It would only cause gossip amongst the servants and alert Sophie to our suspicions.'

'Then what shall we do?'

'I don't know.' Clarissa wrung her hands together. 'If my reasoning is correct then Marianne didn't pack her own portmanteau on the morning you missed her.' The girl tried to follow her sister's trail in logical steps. 'If she were not here that morning, and you did tell me her bed hadn't been slept in, then she must have disappeared on the previous day.'

'She ate her luncheon with me. There was nothing in her manner then to suggest anything was wrong. Indeed, she was looking forward to the Farthingales' ball. She particularly wanted to purchase some lace to decorate up one of her gowns, as I remember.'

'She went out in the afternoon?'

'Yes. To the Emporium, I believe.'

'She would have taken Sophie?'

'Of course. Even if Emily had gone with her, their maids would have accompanied them.'

'Was Emily with her?'

'I don't know, my dear.' Eleanor's eyes narrowed. 'I think we need to question Sophie more closely.'

'No, Aunt.' Clarissa made her views plain. 'I've already interrogated her without success, but I don't think she was telling me the truth, or not the full truth anyway. Does she know Marianne had a twin sister?'

'Very likely. The two of them were closer than I should have liked. I often heard them giggling together while Marianne was getting dressed.'

'Then she must know. She's been suspicious of my role on more than one occasion. I think she thought me convinced of her innocence, but my questions will have alerted her, and I am more than ever sure that Marianne disappeared on that very afternoon.'

'Why?'

'I suspected she'd missed the Farthingales' ball the moment you told me that neither you, nor her friends, had seen her there. You left early, but I dare swear her friends didn't. It didn't seem of any particular note when everyone was convinced she left this house of her own free will on the following morning. It would, however, be unlike my sister to miss the ball if she was able to attend.'

'If she disappeared in the afternoon, then Sophie would have known what happened to her.'

'Exactly! Marianne must have written the note from wherever she ended up that day, which Sophie then delivered to you with a suitable story to prevent suspicion falling upon herself.'

'Marianne must have been kidnapped,' Eleanor gasped, with a sudden stab of apprehension.

'If so, there's been no ransom request,' noted Clarissa calmly. 'Moreover, since everyone seems to concur in considering Sophie devoted to my sister, it's unlikely she'd remain silent if her mistress were taken against her will. It's still my belief that Marianne did indeed leave of her own accord, though for what reason, I can't even begin to speculate.'

'Perhaps she was injured, even killed. One hears so much about these dreadful gangs of Mohawks.'

'If she were injured, then Sophie would have been the first to bring aid to her,' Clarissa calmed her aunt's fears. 'If she were dead, then why not say so?' She thought a moment, wondering if such a death could have implicated the maid. 'No, it cannot be,' she decided. 'When I first arrived at your house Sophie truly did believe I was Marianne, of that I'm sure. She was surprised to see me, but not so shocked that I could have returned from the dead. I doubt whether Marianne would have ventured anywhere she might encounter Mohawks, in any case.' Privately Clarissa doubted that her aunt actually knew what a Mohawk was, and indeed, she had no great idea herself.

'If Sophie knows where Marianne is, then we must ask Downing to bring her to us,' decided Aunt Eleanor finally.

'No. She won't talk unless she believes Marianne is truly in danger.'

'She will if I send Edward down to Bow Street,' declared Eleanor. 'The Runners will soon convince her to speak, or have her clapped up in gaol.'

'Which will precipitate exactly the sort of scandal you hoped to avoid in the first place.' Clarissa saw the rejoinder had hit home and pressed her advantage. 'If my reasoning is correct then Sophie knows exactly where my sister is to be found. If Marianne didn't pack her own bags, then you can be sure

Sophie did it for her. Marianne, whatever her circumstances, must need clothes to wear. When was Sophie's last half day?'

'That very morning.' Eleanor had the answer off pat. 'I remember it well. Once I'd read the note I had to invent the story of Marianne's illness on the spot, and when Sophie requested a half day to visit her sick mother I could hardly refuse. With Marianne dispatched to the country to recuperate, there was no reason to deny the girl.'

Clarissa nodded. Sophie would have packed suitable clothing for Marianne and very likely delivered them personally. Clarissa was quite satisfied in her own mind that she'd succeeded in unravelling what had happened, but why and where still remained a complete mystery.

'Was Marianne unhappy?' she asked.

'Of course not,' her aunt replied at once. 'She loved the parties even more than you do.'

'Something must have caused her to leave.'

'Oh, well. I dare say Leighton didn't help.'

'Leighton! I can't see her running away from him. They were to be betrothed.' Clarissa dismissed this out of hand.

'I don't think her affections were that much engaged. It was a brilliant match, of course, for he is very rich and owns vast estates, but for all of that it was a marriage of convenience for them both.' Eleanor stared at Clarissa almost challengingly. 'I have thought recently that you were more suited to Lord Leighton than your sister. He has a decided partiality for you.'

Clarissa chose to ignore the barb in her comment. 'Marianne came to London to make such a match. To have caught the eye of Lord Leighton in her first season is hardly a reason for flight.'

'I had thought that Leighton might have frightened her.'

'So you told me before. I think it most unlikely.' Following the events at Richmond she could feel the heat in her face and decided to leave the matter there for the time being. She intended to discover the reason behind her sister's disappearance in the very near future, and that from Marianne herself.

Sophie was due a further half day on the following afternoon, and Clarissa decided to follow her. Since her sister wasn't likely to be doing her own washing, it was a fair assumption Sophie had been instructed to keep her supplied with clean linen and if her deductions were correct then the maid would lead her directly to her sister. This was information she had no intention of divulging to her aunt; that lady was only too likely to veto such a scheme and she couldn't envisage anyone else taking on the task so successfully.

Clarissa retired to the library and thought long and hard about what her aunt had told her. She knew from discussions with Emily which Emporium was Marianne's favourite. If she and her maid had attended that establishment on the afternoon she disappeared then they wouldn't have been walking, nor was she likely to have taken a public conveyance when the Markhams had their own vehicles in the mews behind their house.

She'd visited the stable block once or twice since arriving in London, each time selecting a sturdy hack to ride. She wasn't as fond of riding as Marianne, but had enjoyed the exercise nevertheless. If the coachman had been busy, as seemed more than likely, then one of the grooms would have driven Marianne and Sophie to the fashionable Emporium and she decided to act immediately.

'Ah, Mr Harricot.' She caught the man who ran their stables on his way up the yard.

'Yes, miss.'

'I wish a carriage to be made ready for me. A closed carriage. Send it around to the front as soon as you may. Oh,' – she tried to make it sound as though she'd only just thought of the matter – 'one of the grooms drove me when I last went to the Emporium. He drove very well, and there is no need to disturb the coachman. I won't be going far.'

'That would be young Tom, miss.'

'Then send him.'

Mr Harricot paused undecided. It wasn't wise to go against the wishes of the fancy, but neither was it prudent to lay himself open to censure by the master. 'I ain't sure about that, miss. Tom could have been dismissed without a reference if the master found out what happened on that occasion. Ay, and me too, for not telling on the boy.'

'Found out what, Harricot?' Clarissa put on her best impression of the grande dame.

'About you not travelling home with your maid, miss.'

'And what do you know of that?' Clarissa was exultant that her theories should be proven so quickly, but worried that Marianne's disappearance might still be made public.

'Ain't no use in bamming me with such stories as you may be sure young Tom did. It ain't right, and no more do I believe you met your particular friends like he says. It were a man you were meeting and I'm surprised in Lord Leighton to think he should have arranged such an assignation. With him being such a nice gentleman an' all.'

The revelation hit home immediately and Clarissa wondered why she hadn't thought of it herself. Marianne went out with only her maid for company and driven by a groom she could apparently trust. Very likely it was, as Harricot suspected, a tryst, and the girl immediately found her thoughts flying back to Marianne's final letter. She'd mentioned a lad, Stephen, wasn't it? Had she run off with him after all? Harricot had no doubt tricked the groom into a partial confession, or more likely, beat it out of him. Then, putting two and two together, mistakenly arrived at Leighton as the villain of the piece.

'Mr Harricot.' Convinced that the lad could provide her with vital clues to her sister's disappearance, Clarissa drew herself to her full height and prepared to overawe the man. 'Let me remind you of my position. If I will it, Tom will drive me, whatever you say or do.'

'Not unless Mr Markham gives his personal authority.'

Clarissa almost stamped her foot when Harricot maintained his surly refusal in the face of her insistence.

'If I have to fetch my uncle—' She didn't have time to complete her threat before Mr Harricot interrupted her once more, which was probably a good thing since her thoughts were so chaotic she'd probably have been betrayed into a quite unladylike indiscretion.

'Mr Markham, miss,' he told her politely. 'He's heading this way.'

'Uncle.' Clarissa ran off to intercept the rapidly approaching gentleman out of Harricot's earshot. 'I really must have Tom as my groom again.' She shouted out the words for the benefit of Mr Harricot. Then, added her reasons in a low tone only her uncle could catch, 'Tom may know more of Marianne than any of us guess. He was driving her on that fateful afternoon.'

'Yes, of course.' John Markham eyed his niece uneasily. He'd had a disturbing interview with his wife, who'd disclosed her own feeling the girl was on course to let an entire litter of cats out of the bag. Thus, when he'd seen her head for the stables, he'd naturally followed. He couldn't quite reconcile the idea of Clarissa, by far the quieter than her sister, revealing all in front of the servants, but he did know just how much their own consequence would suffer if it became common knowledge they'd attempted to fool society. Then again, he'd already discovered that the girl, despite her sweet nature, could prove remarkably stubborn, especially where her sister's well-being was concerned.

'Then it's all right with you, sir.' Mr Harricot eyed his master askance, but turned willingly enough to seek out the young groom when Markham returned a curt word of command.

'Be careful what you say to the lad,' Mr Markham hissed the words out the side of his mouth and straight away turned on his heels. He didn't want to be involved in her machinations.

CHAPTER NINE

A Groom's Tale

'Thank you, Mr Harricot.' The man had accompanied the carriage around to the front of the house and promptly opened the door of the vehicle when Clarissa appeared at the head of the front steps. She was neatly dressed in a pale blue kerseymere travelling suit over gaitered half boots, and displayed a Russian bonnet atop her softly flowing curls, which had been caught up into a knot.

He bowed slightly when she entered the vehicle. 'Ain't you taking your maid, miss?'

'I left behind a trinket I particularly wished to wear. She will be down with it in a moment.' Clarissa was amazed at the facility with which she could tell the lie, and all without the slightest of blushes.

'Yes, miss.' Mr Harricot paused a moment, somewhat over-set by the circumstances. 'I hope you won't hold my refusal against me, miss. I was only doing my duty.'

'I can assure you nothing was further from my mind.' Clarissa closed the door firmly and leaned through the opening with a reassuring smile. 'You may leave with an easy mind, Mr Harricot. Tom is quite capable of holding the horses until Sophie appears.'

'Yes, miss.'

Mr Harricot still showed no signs of leaving until Clarissa raised her eyebrows expressively.

'It's like this, miss,' he began eventually, 'Tom's my own lad and—'

'He won't get into any trouble on my account,' she interrupted him. 'I have no intention of meeting anyone today. I may purchase a few trifling gee-gaws at the Emporium, but I'll be back soon.'

With that Mr Harricot had to be satisfied. He had been dismissed, and though he still plainly harboured suspicions, or at least some anxiety for his son's well-being, he couldn't very well remain in direct defiance of her order.

Clarissa watched after him, waiting until he'd disappeared from view before dismounting from the carriage.

'Hello, Tom,' she began, to put him at his ease. 'I seem to owe you something of an apology. I understand you could have been turned off without reference for allowing me to slip the traces.'

'Yes, miss.' The lad turned a pair of bright eyes on her. 'Wasn't you, though, was it, miss?'

'It wasn't?' Clarissa resorted to acting like the proverbial parrot, so surprised as she was at having her deception discovered by a boy she'd barely met.

'You're very like her, but you're not Miss Marianne.'

Clarissa floundered for a moment longer, then decided it wasn't worth the effort in trying to confound his theories.

'No,' she answered wearily. 'How did you guess?'

'Miss Marianne always took Sabre out when she wished to ride. He's a bit of a handful when fresh, and you prefer a quieter mount. Pleased my da no end.' Tom paused shyly. 'Mr Harricot, that is. He thought you were showing proper decorum for once, but it suspicioned me. Then again, when you returned from the country, Miss Sophie asked me some very strange questions about where you'd suddenly appeared from and who'd collected you. Not like her to dally with the stable lads, miss. She's no flighty young maid like some I could name. Miss Sophie's proper hoity toity.'

'You're a very clever young lad.' Clarissa considered her groom carefully, wondering how she could deal with the situation.

'I ain't seeking to make it difficult for you, miss. I won't tell on you.' He gave her a searching glance. 'Not if you're looking to help Miss Marianne. Is she still unwell?'

'She disappeared on the very afternoon you brought Sophie home without her.' Clarissa, having considered the matter, decided to confide in the stable lad. 'Nobody's seen her since, though she did leave a note to say she'd return as soon as she might. The Markhams put around news of her illness and subsequent retirement to the country to protect her from ill-mannered gossip.'

She watched a gamut of emotions play across the young lad's face and instantly decided he must have been totally under Marianne's spell. No doubt a pawn in his position would have been a useful adjunct to her sister when she was planning an illicit tryst.

'I didn't want to leave without her,' the young groom admitted, 'but Miss Sophie told me it was all above board and I knew she wouldn't let any harm come to her beloved mistress. Was it Lord Leighton she met?'

'I doubt it. Did you see no one?'

'No, miss. I stayed with the carriage while they took a stroll on one of the commons. Only a small one, miss, not like the fashionable parks.' He gave a start. 'Are you a detective, miss?'

'No.' Clarissa had to laugh despite her fears. 'I'm her sister and beginning to get worried for her safety. She might have written that she'd return, but she hasn't done so yet.'

'What do you want from me?'

'Was she ... did she have any luggage with her that after-noon?'

'Not that I was aware of,' the lad answered at once. 'She certainly carried nothing when she went walking, and later, once Sophie returned, she never went after her with any baggage.'

That, at least, seemed to scotch any suspicion of an elope-ment. Marianne wouldn't have been such a goose as to forget her luggage. Nevertheless, Clarissa felt certain her sister had gone to the park with the specific intention of meeting someone, in all probability a man.

'Do you know anyone called Stephen?' Clarissa threw in the name at random, it was the only lead she had. 'Marianne or Sophie might have mentioned his name in passing.'

'No, miss.' He paused of a sudden and wrinkled his brows. 'Now you mention baggage, miss, I saw Sophie early next morning when she tried to sneak out the back alleyway loaded down with a huge bundle. The rear gate is approached past the stables and I happened to be working outside that morning. She told me Miss Marianne had allowed her to take some old blankets to her sister who was sick, but if what you tell me is true, then Miss Marianne never returned and she was telling me a lie.'

'She was lying to you,' Clarissa decided. 'Are you sure she was only carrying blankets?'

'No, miss, I didn't think no more of it at the time. I had other things to occupy my mind than what secrets a maidservant was carrying. Mr Harricot was in a rare temper with me, and he owns a heavy hand when he's mad.' Tom positively blanched when he remembered the incident. 'The bundle was certainly wrapped in a blanket, but what it contained I couldn't say for certain.'

'It was early?'

'Yes, miss. It'd be before breakfast, at any rate, and we break our fast early in the stables.'

'Could she have carried the bundle as far as you'd driven?'

'Easily, miss,' replied the young groom scornfully. 'Miss Sophie's strong as an ox.'

'You may drive me there then.' Clarissa made the decision on the instant. She had to make a journey or Mr Harricot would become suspicious, if no one else, and if her sister hadn't eloped then Marianne, in all likelihood, would remain close by her trysting place.

'What about your maid?'

'Sophie won't be joining us.'

'I suspicioned that, but it ain't right for you to travel about without her,' Tom told her firmly.

'Neither would I, if I weren't so anxious for Miss Marianne.'

Using her sister's name seemed to remove the lad's final objection to her scheme, though he refused to be totally silenced. 'Mr Harricot will kill me if he hears of this,' he muttered.

'Then don't tell him,' advised the damsel, who was beginning to think herself sunk completely beyond reproach.

The journey itself was unexpectedly short. No more than ten minutes, though, as Clarissa fully realized, it would have taken much longer to walk and she didn't envy Sophie her task in carrying an apparently large bundle over such a distance. Neither was it anywhere near any Emporium she knew of. She stared at her new surroundings with a jaundiced eye and categorized her findings.

They were parked by the kerb of a wide crescent, flanked on

one side with neatly kept housing and the other by a wide arena of greensward enclosed by iron railings, echoing, in form if not beauty, the elegant gardens that fronted the Markham residence. The houses themselves, though sufficiently large to preserve a feeling of wealth, didn't display the same elevated taste as those in the Markhams' own square. She decided they were probably the homes of well-off tradespeople; not those of the wealthiest classes, who were rich as Croesus and could afford to ape the excesses of the aristocracy, but merchants who were nevertheless both successful and respectable.

Marianne had evidently walked in the park, and even through the carriage window, Clarissa could see the tracks that meandered across the grass, some of them disappearing into the bushes and trees that marked the far edge of the meadow-land at no great distance.

'Miss Marianne went off in that direction.' Tom suddenly appeared on the edge of her vision, one hand holding on to the reins and the other pointing out a path that led into the thickest of the vegetation. 'They disappeared for quite a time, a couple of hours at least, but at long length Miss Sophie came back alone.' He hung his head. 'I suspicioned Miss Marianne was meeting someone she shouldn't, not in secret anyways.'

'Didn't you question Sophie when she returned?'

'She told me Miss Marianne had met some of her friends. They were all going to the party together.'

'Without her clothes, or her maid?'

'I didn't think of that at the time,' responded the groom. 'No one in the house seemed worried for her, or I might have brought it up before I told my Da next day. Made him madder than a hornet, but it didn't seem to signify. By that time we'd already been told how Miss Marianne was driven into the country to recover from a fever.'

'You were told it was a fever she suffered from?' Clarissa wondered how any of the servants had been duped by such an unimaginative tale. 'What did your father think of that story?'

'I never noticed no fever.' The lad turned wide, innocent eyes on his mistress and she interpolated the rest.

Aunt Eleanor may have thought she was fooling everyone, but the servants had obviously been talking. Society too, if what she'd heard of the gossip from Emily was to be believed. Her face flushed when she realized on what a knife edge she'd stood; only her remarkable likeness to her sister could have saved the day. And even that may not have sufficed if Leighton's attentions hadn't been so particular. Was that a deliberate ploy on his part? Had he, too, suspected something was in the wind? Visiting the Markhams so immediately on his return pointed towards such a suspicion, but finding her in residence must have forestalled his uncertainty.

Clarissa was quite sure in her deception; no one but Sophie and the stable lad had reason to be suspicious of her role as Marianne. Both of them, for their own reasons, were absurdly loyal to her sister; loyal to the point of abetting her in an undertaking that could ruin her future forever.

Tom, at least, seemed to realize how wrong he'd been and Clarissa threw herself on his conscience.

'Sophie has a half day due, this very afternoon,' she told him earnestly. 'I believe she knows exactly where to find Miss Marianne, and if I'm correct, she may take the opportunity to visit her. I intend to follow her.'

'On foot, miss? I don't think that's such a good idea.'

The young lad looked as though he were out of his depth, and to prevent him confessing the whole to his father, Clarissa issued a stern warning.

'It wasn't a good idea to keep quiet about my sister's whereabouts either, my lad. You, and your father too, both of you could lose your jobs over this, and very likely face a spell in gaol, if you aren't transported first.' The young groom paled, close to tears, and Clarissa softened her expression. 'Help me, and I swear you won't regret it.'

'I'll come with you, miss,' he assented eagerly.

'No.' Clarissa was very clear. 'I'll follow her on my own. The pair of us together will create more interest than a single lady alone.'

'Then what do you want from me?'

'Sophie will leave by the servant's entrance around the side of the house. I can engage to spot her if she exits into the square; the morning-room overlooks the street at the front. If she decides to sneak out of the rear gates as she did before then I'd never know. You must keep that way under observation and send a message to me if she attempts it.'

'Yes, miss.' The young groom wasn't satisfied with the role Clarissa had mapped out, but neither did he intend to question a lady who'd already shown a hint of the steel in her. His most pressing problem would lie in sending a message to the young mistress without raising suspicions; his da really would kill him if he discovered his son aiding her in yet another illicit adventure.

CHAPTER TEN

Lost in the Capital

Fortunately for Clarissa the Markhams were both out visiting during the day, and she was able to bespeak an early luncheon before stationing herself in a window embrasure in the morning-room. Doubly fortunate, for either one of her relatives would have exclaimed at her costume, and even Downing, who'd served her lunch, had found the steady nerves of a butler almost over-set. For, in the expectation of needing to look somewhat less of the lady of fashion, Clarissa had donned one of the dowdiest of the gardening clothes she herself had brought with her. The costume was neat and clean, of course, but nothing could disguise its unfashionable cut or threadbare appearance. Nevertheless it would more nearly suit her intentions to merge into the background during her self-imposed task of following her maid, than any other of her gowns.

Despite her fears that Sophie would slip into the alleyway through the rear entrance to the Markhams' grounds, the maid dutifully appeared on the street in front of Clarissa's own eyes later that afternoon. That young lady immediately leapt up, and catching hold of an equally unfashionable spencer and poke bonnet to hide her hair, hared down the stairs and through the front door before a bemused footman had the chance to open it for her.

She'd made no note of the maidservant's direction, but to her relief Sophie was still in plain sight and she settled down to follow the girl. It was a simple task at first, the wide avenues, crescents and squares of the more fashionable streets allowing her to hang back out of plain sight. These, however, soon gave way to poorer districts, and Clarissa found herself having to close in on her quarry for fear of losing her in the maze of roads and alleyways she found herself following. The carriage had not travelled this route, but she decided it must be a short cut. She certainly hoped so, for London was proving to be bigger and dirtier than she could ever have imagined in her wildest dreams.

About this time she began to suspect that either Sophie knew she was being followed and was attempting to lose her pursuer, or that they were heading for a totally different part of town from that in which Tom had dropped her sister. The maid ducked into a maze of filthy alleyways with all the confidence of a local and Clarissa followed, breaking into a trot, for she was determined by now to catch her quarry and have it out with her whatever the cost. Marianne would never have consented to remain in a place like this!

They turned a corner, almost tunnel like in its proportions, with Clarissa no more than a couple of yards behind, but to her surprise, the maid had vanished. Astonished by the swift disappearance of her quarry, the girl stared perplexed at the rubbish-strewn street and the stinking miasma that rose from its filthy surface. Only one doorway seemed to fit the circumstances and Clarissa immediately grasped its handle and strode in, expecting to find Sophie had taken refuge in a shop.

She was wrong; it was a common ale-house, if such a stinking, smoke-ridden, vermin-infested hole could be dignified by that appellation. The customers were as dirty and unsavoury as the hell-hole itself and Clarissa speedily backed out when one of them shouted out a very blunt and distasteful invitation. She stared around herself again, aware the maidservant had tricked her, but without any clear plan forming in her mind. Had Sophie braved the disgusting odours of the ale-house? Or was she hiding somewhere close by? The ale-house door began to open, and the burly rough who'd issued the lewd invitation appeared. Clarissa fled.

At first she thought she was retracing her steps, but it soon became clear she was only thrusting deeper into the filthy streets of the poorest and roughest of districts. A wider avenue, along which a street market was operating, brought hope to her breast and she began to stride out, shrinking from the beggars and other roughs squatting in the filth of the gutters.

'Please.' She accosted one of the least mean-looking of a band of women gathered around the entrance to a dark and gloomy alleyway.

'What d'you mean by coming round 'ere, you painted little madam? Go find your own pitch.' The woman's face swiftly turned as ugly as her threats and Clarissa backed off, uneasily aware of the filthy names being flung at her by the other women. It was a misunderstanding, but she was wise enough not to stay to explain it, when some of the suggestions for her immediate disposal involved painful and anatomically impossible adjustments to her body.

She ran on in a panic, following the wider avenues, until at length she came upon the edge of a commercial district. Evening was beginning to fall and since not one of the people on the streets looked in the slightest bit respectable, Clarissa began to realize she could expect no help from any quarter. She was lost and would have to find herself.

For a moment she floundered then, catching a glimpse of the river, began to orient herself. She knew she must travel west, upriver, but stared at the rapidly darkening, jumble of streets and alleyways in that direction with some dismay. A young girl careered out of a side road and cannoned into her, knocking them both headlong into a filthy puddle that stained the gutters. A burly man was following her at a run, hurling a stream of foul invective and whirling the crop in his hand.

Her clothing muddy and dirt stained, Clarissa hauled herself to her feet, wincing when the man began to beat the poor girl, who could do no more than wail piteously while attempting to dodge his blows.

'Cease that at once, sir,' she demanded imperiously, and bravely stepped in to stop the beating.

'You filthy doxy,' the man began, looking her up and down with disdain. 'Leave us alone, or I'll let you have a taste of the whip, too.' He stepped forward and raised his crop threateningly.

Clarissa stood proud, giving him the pause, but before it could be seen whether he'd carry out his threat or not, a curricle, hauled by no less than four steaming horses, skidded to a halt and a tall rangy figure leapt out.

'Richard!' Clarissa stared at the apparition in amazement, watching open mouthed while he plucked the crop from her opponent's nerveless fingers.

'Damn you, sir,' that worthy told him, swiftly recovering from the surprise of his arrival. And attempted a right cross that would have taken Leighton's head off if it had landed.

Lord Leighton had boxed at Cribb's Parlour for as long as he'd been on the Town, so it was no surprise to him that he should slip the punch and return it with interest. A punishing left hook under the short ribs staggered the man and brought him up short, followed by a right to the point of the chin that finished the business. Clarissa was left bemused when her erstwhile attacker dropped to the ground as though pole-axed.

'Come, Marianne,' – Leighton took her hand and drew her back – 'and tell me' – his brows rose with pardonable inquisitiveness – 'why should such a man seek to attack you?'

'Not me, Richard.' Clarissa was beginning to gather her scattered wits. 'He was chasing her.' She pointed out the girl he'd been whipping, but who was now standing guard over the man's prone figure with a feral snarl on her face.

'Ah. A domestic tiff, I presume.' In the aftermath of the action, Leighton had regained his sang-froid with remarkable speed. He indicated the curricle with a wave of his hand and Clarissa recognized his matched bays.

'Thank you, sir.' She leaned on the support of his hand and hauled herself on to the sporting carriage with relief.

'Let them go, lad.' Leighton had leapt up beside her and spoken to his tiger. Only it wasn't his tiger, and Clarissa felt a sense of foreboding. The lad holding the horses was none other than Tom, whom she thought to have left at the house. How much of her story had he divulged to Leighton?

The journey home was short, but fraught with embarrassment. Lord Leighton not unnaturally wanted an explanation, but before she would venture to give one, she had a question of her own.

'How did you find me, Richard?'

'Tom was lucky enough to find me at home.'

'Tom?'

'I have yet to find the bottom of matters, but apparently he was following in your footsteps when you found yourself lost in the back streets. He in turn lost you, and realizing I was the closest of any who might protect you, came to knock me up. We've been searching for a couple of hours. You might start by telling me why your groom should be following you.'

'I don't know,' Clarissa quavered, miserably aware that her answer was unsatisfactory. Damn the lad, she hadn't asked him to follow her. Then immediately she regretted her uncharitable thoughts. She'd still be lost, and probably have been beaten into the bargain, if he hadn't thought to protect her.

'Not good enough, Marianne.'

Leighton's voice sounded severe and Clarissa shivered when she looked up into his face. It was a tight mask that told of the anger bubbling beneath. This wasn't the moment to tell the truth, not when it could spell the end of Marianne's career in society. Neither could she bear to see the hurt in her beloved's face when he learned how thoroughly they'd deceived him. He'd be angry too, but that she could bear; she knew she deserved it.

'I believed my maidservant was acting dishonestly,' she temporized. 'I had no proof of the matter, but I saw her make off with some clothing and straight away made the decision to follow after her.' Clarissa prayed Tom had said nothing to the contrary. 'Young Tom must have seen me leave the house and thought it sufficiently odd in me to follow.' She paused and risked a peek at Leighton's face, aware that he didn't believe a word of her story. 'It was very good of him to do so.'

'Good indeed. I see you managed to find the time to change your clothes, too. I presume the gown you're wearing, hideous as it is, would be more appropriate to such an adventure.'

'I was about to address some minor task in the garden.' Clarissa could have sunk into the ground. Of all the people to find her in her rags, he was the last she would have chosen. Then she immediately amended her thoughts; he'd done her a great service in finding her.

'Don't try my patience, Marianne.' She could see that Leighton had put the lid on his anger, but it still showed in his speech. 'Your conduct in disappearing so abruptly from society caused a lot of careless talk, but, more importantly, left me worried that our betrothal wasn't to your taste. Our meetings since your return suggested I'd been mistaken, and when you returned my kisses at Richmond, I told myself no one could have faked such emotion.'

Clarissa's face flared at his reminder of her foolishness. How dare he fling her passionate response back at her? Hadn't he been the one to kiss her? Then the truth struck home: he still had the power to make her long for his embrace, to desire the searing sensation of his kisses. If only he would take her in his arms right away. Her blushes consumed her, and she hung her head in shame.

'I'm sorry, Richard,' she told him a small voice. 'I can't tell you why I was following Sophie.' She laid a hand on his arm, a plea for his forgiveness. 'Not now, not ever! But please believe me, it is not for the sake of some thoughtless whim. I love you.'

The truth was in her eyes and Leighton felt his heart melt. 'I won't press you for an explanation now, my dear,' he advised her gently, 'but I won't stand for such secrecy after we're married, and so I warn you.'

'There'll be no need for concern once our vows have been exchanged,' she reassured him.

'Thank you.' Leighton enclosed her hand in his and tooled the open carriage up the Markhams' street with a very pretty piece of one handed driving.

'Will you come in, Richard?' Clarissa made the polite request.

'I believe Mr Markham has returned from his visit. Indeed, both my aunt and uncle would be pleased to see you.'

'No, thank you, Marianne. I have a pleasant little party of my own planned for tonight. I should, however, be pleased to pass on an invitation from my sister to visit her tomorrow afternoon.' He paused, before announcing gravely. 'I shall be there myself.'

'I should love to.' Clarissa could see the simple joy she felt in the invitation had been communicated to him and felt a moment of apprehension. Should she be torturing herself by accepting? Torturing *him*, perhaps? She already felt she loved his sister too, but what use was that when both he and his sister would soon be related to Marianne, and not herself? On the other hand she knew she had to accept if she were to continue in her role, but how, oh how she wished it was really her he was inviting, and not her sister.

CHAPTER ELEVEN

Sophie's Escape

'Good morning, miss.' Sophie slowly peeled back the curtains at the window when her mistress began to stir.

Clarissa stared at her maid in amazement. Following the events of the previous day she hadn't ever expected to see the girl again, let alone find her going about her allotted tasks as though nothing had happened.

'Sophie?' She began to question her own senses, shaking her head and rubbing the sleep out of her eyes.

'Yes, miss.' The girl turned wide, innocent eyes on her. 'Are you planning to go out this morning?'

'Yes, Sophie. I'm engaged to visit Lady Burnett.' Clarissa retreated into the common-place while she considered the matter, beginning to wonder if the girl had spotted her at all the previous afternoon. Could it have been mere coincidence that she'd been lured into the murky depths of the city stews? Her maidservant had seemed at home in the narrow alleyways. Perhaps she was visiting her family just as she had promised.

'While you're washing, I'll set out your morning gown, miss. The one with the pale-blue stripe.'

'Thank you, Sophie.' Clarissa flung her legs out of bed and

strode across to the dressing-table where she splashed a generous measure of steaming water from a jug into the simple porcelain basin. All her instincts were screaming that Sophie was playing the scene far too casually to be entirely innocent. That being so, had she deliberately led her mistress into a dangerous situation? Or had she just been desperate to lose her? Either way, it implied the maidservant had something to hide and, to Clarissa's way of thinking, whatever it was would explain her sister's disappearance.

She considered her next move carefully. For Marianne's sake as much as her own, she couldn't risk society, even her particular friends, discovering her deception, but neither could she afford to continue to deceive Richard much longer. She'd already decided she wouldn't allow herself to be betrothed to him in place of her sister. It wouldn't be fair to entrap him if Marianne failed to return in time for the grand ball her uncle and aunt had arranged in their honour. And that ball was scheduled for less than a fortnight hence. The mystery must be solved before that date, or she would confess all and sink herself beyond reproach, a painful outcome she was determined to avoid.

'Sophie.' She decided on the direct approach, hoping to catch her maidservant on the hop. 'Where is Marianne?'

'Marianne, miss?' Sophie stared at Clarissa as though she was mad, but there'd been a moment of indecision in her voice that revealed the truth to her mistress. The girl was lying.

'I'm not Marianne, as you very well know,' Clarissa explained. 'Your mistress went missing weeks ago, when she was in your company.' That last piece of information was an inspired guess flung at random, but failed to win any appreciable response from the girl.

'No, miss, I don't know, really I don't.' Sophie's eyes stared wide at her accuser, round as saucers. 'My mistress gone missing, when you're here? Why, you're funning with me, aren't you miss?' The maidservant made a passable attempt at a giggle, but Clarissa didn't allow herself to be fooled by such a display of spurious innocence.

'You knew me for an impostor the very first day we met. How? Aren't we enough alike to pass muster?'

Sophie compressed her lips and stared back in silence. There was no point in dissemblance, only dumb insolence would do.

'What did I say that made you suspicious?' Clarissa knew her resemblance to her twin was remarkable and that she could even give a passable impression of Marianne's more volatile personality. Yet the maid had found her out within a minute of meeting her.

Sophie continued to stare at her with a sulky expression. 'I don't know what you mean, miss. I ain't never been suspicious. Not of you.' She edged towards the door. 'Mr Downing told me to get back down to the kitchen soon as you're dressed. He don't like to be kept waiting.'

Clarissa made a sudden dive for the bedroom door and barred her maid's exit. For a moment they stared, eyeball to eyeball, until eventually the maidservant looked away. Moving deliberately, Clarissa carefully turned the key in the lock and removed it.

'I'm not yet dressed.'

'No, miss.'

'Where's my sister? What have you done with her?' Clarissa resisted an overwhelming urge to slap the girl.

'Your sister, miss? Ain't she with your aunt? Your other aunt, I mean, the one what lives in the country, not Mrs Markham.' Sophie had set herself to reply in the negative, and Clarissa knew a moment of panic until she saw the fear reflected in the girl's eyes.

'You know better than that. I also believe you know where Marianne is to be found.'

'Well, if you ain't Miss Marianne, miss, then who are you?' The maid's voice turned ragged, as though she, too, was at the end of her tether.

'Sophie, please help me.' Clarissa, who was becoming desperate, tried her hardest to ingratiate herself with the girl. 'I only want to find Marianne. Not harm her. She's my sister, and I'm so worried for her safety. Please tell me she's not imprisoned, or lying hurt.'

'No need for you to worry, miss.' Sophie sounded sympathetic for an instant, but once she realized the complicity her words implied, began to wish she'd bitten off her tongue.

'What I mean is,' she continued, 'I never realized you weren't Marianne. How could I have? You're so alike. Mind you, I thought it proper strange when she disappeared so suddenly. I never did believe in the stories the master and mistress put out about her illness.' She made a plausible attempt at innocence, and endeavoured to end on a note of pert jocularity. 'La, my own mistress packed off to the country without a word said to me.'

'If you failed to realize I was playing a part, how come you led me such a dance yesterday?' Clarissa knew she'd scored a direct hit with the question. Sophie had started perceptibly.

'I'd taken some of Marianne's—' She stared at her mistress fearfully. 'Taken some of your clothes.' Her voice picked up in confidence as her story unfolded. 'I stole them, miss, to my shame. I thought you'd discovered me and were giving chase.'

'You were taking the clothes to Marianne.'

'No, miss. Indeed not. I needed the money. Honest. My mother's proper ill and we don't have enough money to pay for her doctoring what with Dad being laid off at the docks.'

'There's no need to lie to me, Sophie. We're both on the same side, Marianne's side. I know how much you love my sister. I do too. But she must return to her own world. Please. At least tell me whether she's in good health. She isn't hurt, is she? Or held captive?'

'No, miss, really. She's in fine health. Never better.' Sophie suddenly broke down under Clarissa's eloquence. 'But she don't want to come back here, leastways not yet.'

'Where is she?'

'I can't tell you, miss.' The girl began to sob and Clarissa fought to hold her baser instincts in check. Shaking the girl until her teeth rattled might relieve her feelings, but it would ultimately get her nowhere.

'Sophie, you must. You really must.' She kept her voice calm while she pleaded her case.

'No, miss.' Sophie's face had assumed an expression of stubborn sulkiness and Clarissa decided reinforcements were needed.

'I'll fetch Mr Markham,' she threatened. 'He'll know what to do with you. If you try to hide her whereabouts from him, it'll be Bow Street and an interview with the Runners for you.'

Clarissa shrank from putting this threat into operation, but the maidservant remained adamant in her refusal to speak, leaving her no option but to summon the Markhams to her aid. She turned the key in the lock, slipped out of the room and carefully relocked the door.

Mr Markham would undoubtedly be busy in his study at this hour, but Clarissa had no intention of seeking him out. She was wearing no more than a thin night rail, and had no wish to be discovered by one of the male servants in such a skimpy costume, nor by her uncle either. Mrs Markham's quarters were only a couple of doors down the corridor and, unlike her busy husband, her aunt would still be lying abed.

'Aunt Eleanor.' Clarissa didn't scruple to break in on her aunt whom she found propped up on her pillows poring over her correspondence. 'Sophie has admitted all.' She began her explanation without ceremony and with scant regard for her aunt's sensibilities. 'I believe she knows exactly where Marianne is situated, but I can't make her tell me.'

'Clarissa!' Eleanor stared transfixed at the picture of her niece's skimpy wardrobe, while she considered how she should react.

'Only come quick, Aunt. Never mind your dress. I don't dare leave Sophie for too long. She'll only recover herself and deny everything.' Clarissa looked as though she'd rush back to her room without her aunt, and indeed, dismayed by Aunt Eleanor's dithering she'd almost arrived at a decision to seek out her uncle despite her state of dishabille.

'Wait, I'll come with you,' Aunt Eleanor decided at last, ringing for her maid and starting from the bed. 'Where's your robe, child?' she complained. 'You can't roam these corridors with no more clothes than a veritable hoyden would wear.'

'I don't have time to waste on fripperies, Aunt,' her niece replied, with scant ceremony. 'We must tackle Sophie together before she recovers her nerve. You're the mistress in this house, and I'm convinced you need apply very little pressure for her to break down completely. Send your dresser to fetch Mr Markham too. If we two can't frighten her into disclosing Marianne's whereabouts, then I dare say he'll know what to do.'

Clarissa ignored the faint protests her aunt was uttering and raced back down the corridor to unlock her room once more. She stared around the apartment nonplussed. Sophie was no longer there.

Mr Markham arrived at much the same time as his wife, only to find Clarissa staring disconsolately through the open window.

'No sign of her,' she corroborated miserably. 'I should have guessed she'd flee at the first opportunity.'

CHAPTER TWELVE

Leighton Declares Himself

Despite finding her mood sadly lowered in the wake of Sophie's desperate flight, Clarissa resolved to honour her appointment with Lady Burnett. Not only did she regard Caroline as a friend, but Leighton himself would be there. She scolded herself that her spirits should rise so quickly at the very thought of meeting her sister's betrothed, but she couldn't find it within her heart to deny him to herself. Marianne was still lost to her, but though she could pretend it was mere play acting, seeing Richard would bring comfort to her.

'Marianne.' Caroline greeted her with tender regard when she was shown into the elegant and sunny withdrawing-room at the front of the Burnetts' house, holding out her hands and drawing her straight away into a warm embrace. 'Richard is already here, as you see.'

Leighton immediately claimed Clarissa's hand and drew it fondly to his lips, holding on to the embrace a little too long for mere civility. 'My love,' he greeted her with a sparkle in his eyes, seeming to have forgotten the diatribe he'd read her on yesterday's escapades.

'Come, sit by me.' Caroline reclaimed her guest's hand and

drew her down beside herself on a comfortable settle. 'We can have a comfortable prose later, but unfortunately I have to attend to matters in the kitchen in the meantime. Our house-keeper has not yet taken me through today's menus, but there's no need for you to concern yourself, when Richard's here to bear you company.'

Clarissa eyed Leighton anxiously when Caroline left with one last squeeze of her hand. There was no doubt in her mind they'd been left alone on purpose and that it was at the behest of her, or more correctly, Marianne's, soon-to-be-betrothed. No doubt it was a chance to quiz her again about the events of the previous day; in all probability to question her wisdom, or lack of such, in gadding about the capital without a respectable companion.

She'd already held a hurried conference with her groom, Tom, to discover what Leighton had learned from him. If the boy were to be believed, then Richard was in possession of no more than the fact that Tom had followed her because he saw his mistress take off after her maid alone. She determined that would be all he knew, for her own sake as much as Marianne's.

In actual fact, she was much surprised to find he'd more important matters on his mind than her unusual conduct.

'Marianne.' Clarissa looked startled when Richard fell down on one knee at her feet. 'Marianne, you must know I love you more than life itself.' He took hold of the hand he'd so recently released and pressed it to his lips again. 'Please grant me the honour of becoming my wife.'

'Oh, Richard.' Clarissa's heart melted. 'No, oh no, you must get up. Caroline will return.'

'Not yet awhile, beloved,' he replied confidently.

'But—'

'I realize my previous proposal was too formal, and indeed I didn't provide you with all the attention you deserved on that occasion. It is otherwise now.'

Clarissa hadn't been in attendance when last he'd proposed, but she could readily imagine that a suitor offering a marriage of convenience might resort to tedious formality in his offer.

'There is no need to renew your offer, Richard.' She felt an unreasoning embarrassment in his love-making. This was her sister's scene, not hers. If only she could have induced Sophie to betray her whereabouts, Marianne could then have received the repeated offer herself. And in the same moment her eyes began to fill with tears. This was so exactly what she wanted for herself!

'The ball at which we're to be publicly betrothed is drawing closer day by day,' he reminded her. 'It's important to me, to us, that you accept my suit unreservedly, that you realize our marriage is a love match.'

'I've already accepted you once,' she faltered. Despite his plea for love, Clarissa couldn't accept his proposal for herself, she just couldn't. Marianne was the sister he was betrothed to, not her. It would be too cruel to give her love and accept his hand, only to have it torn roughly from her grasp again.

'I beg of you, Marianne. Surely you haven't been so wholly averse to my attentions since I returned from my estates?'

'Oh no, I beg you, no.' Clarissa laid her free hand lightly on his cheek, instinctively drawing him closer with the tender caress. 'I do truly love you, Richard, but you don't, indeed you can't, know the whole.'

She felt an overwhelming desire to throw herself on his mercy, to explain her position, knowing all the while she could do nothing of the sort. For the sake of her sister's honour, perhaps even her safety, she must remain silent. Such a tale would surely give him a disgust of her too, for how could any woman retain any smattering of honour and propriety when she'd shown herself only too willing to take his kisses, and even return them with all the fervour of a lover, when she could never play that part for real.

'Marianne, I don't care for the past. If you love me now—' Lord Leighton deserted words for action. All of a sudden he flung himself to the settle by her side and reached out for her.

One of his hands slid confidently through her curls and cupped her head tenderly, while the other took a firm grip on her waist. His lips swooped down, pressing his advantage, taking her own with all the practised accomplishment of a demon lover. Her senses swirled and her lips parted; and before she knew it, one hand was kneading his muscular shoulder, while the other fluttered as wildly as her willing heart.

'Please, sir.' She tore her lips away and resorted to formality, knowing just how close she'd come to complete abandonment. Her breasts rose and fell to the violence of her breathing and she knew he was as aware of her feelings as though she'd admitted them to him herself. She would be lost if she didn't put an end to the scene immediately.

'Sir, you cannot admit your original offer was made for pure convenience rather than true love, then take my kisses however you wish. We are not yet wed, nor even formally betrothed.' The speech was more stilted than Clarissa was prepared to admit, but it gave her space to compose herself.

'It was a marriage of convenience I once proposed,' he admitted. 'I made no secret that it was done to secure the succession, and neither did you do anything to suggest your feelings were engaged any more than mine.' He stared at her, his chest rising and falling as fast as her own. 'My feelings have long since altered, love has grown, grown so fast my head is left spinning. It's as though I met another woman in you when I returned from inspecting my estates and I could swear that you felt the same. Surely you see that?'

'Yes.' Clarissa spoke quietly, her head hung low. She was speaking from the heart, though she couldn't, for the sake of her sister, speak of all that was in her heart, couldn't pour out her love for the man who was going to marry her sister. Nevertheless, she was in raptures, and for the life of her, she couldn't help but be elated when she knew that Richard had spoken words of love meant for her alone. For Clarissa!

Later, she'd be disappointed, of course. Marianne would return and marry her lord, and surely they'd deal well together. Poor, dowdy Clarissa would die an old maid, or perhaps accept the cleric if he'd still have her. But for now she could drink in the desire she could see in Richard's face, the words of love on his lips, the light touch of his hand on her waist, and know the ecstasy of loving and being loved in return.

'We can be married within a month,' he declared, confident he'd beaten down her opposition.

'Richard.' She felt her face warm with a becoming blush when a gasp parted her lips.

It was too much for any man!

Leighton's head dipped once more and she was lost. Lost to all propriety and any maidenly modesty she may have felt. She turned in his arms, barely aware that her own were clasping him as relentlessly as his held her. She felt the crisp hairs at his nape in her fingers, the bruising rasp of his lips moving against her own, his breath in her mouth. She gasped out loud when, with a cry of desire, he drew her closer, her breasts crushed against the hard contours of his muscular chest, taut and sensitive, sending dimly perceived messages to the most intimate parts of her body. She was all too aware of the strength in his thigh that nestled so comfortably against her own, and shifted her outer leg to lay across it, her soft flesh massaging his muscular length.

His kiss continued to ravage her until she could stand no more and threw back her head to bare her throat. He pounced upon the soft, delicate skin exposed; nipping, sucking, kissing while she writhed beneath his ardour and drank in the soft loving words he whispered into her treacherously receptive ears. She could feel his hands moving on her body and—

They heard the door opening as one, and leapt apart before his sister could enter.

Caroline almost laughed at the dismay evident in their faces, for though she couldn't have imagined the intensity of their feelings, she had expected some sort of love-making to have been in progress. Why else would she have rattled the door knob with such violence.

'I should not have left you along so long,' she declared, pretending not to notice how Clarissa was brushing the creases out of her garments, or of how flushed her face was.

'No matter, I assure you.' Leighton's voice was as urbane as it was polite, but his sister couldn't quite stifle her giggle when she saw the warning glare in his eye. All very well, but even for her brother's sake, she couldn't leave a couple not formally betrothed to their own devices for long. She risked another glance at her future sister-in-law and deduced it had been too long, or, with another stifled giggle, perhaps not long enough. She was grinning like a cheshire cat, for despite her earlier fears for the match, it seemed these two would make the perfect marriage.

Leighton remembered his manners and stood up. 'Sit here, Caroline,' he murmured politely.

'Thank you, Brother.' Caroline gracefully seated herself next to Clarissa, and allowed herself a moment of pure mischief. 'I thought you were sitting over there when I left.'

'Marianne and I had business to attend to.' Leighton had recovered himself as fully as he was likely to under the circumstances. 'We've decided to bring the marriage forward.'

'I should agree that's a wise move,' agreed Caroline, quite unable to stifle her giggles this time.

Clarissa could have sunk through the floor. Caroline, she was convinced, had guessed exactly how badly they'd been behaving, and how should she not? Her own blushes must have told her they hadn't comported themselves with any degree of decorum.

Damn Richard and his words of love. She felt her blushes spread, the heat building further in her face. It wasn't Richard who should be damned, it was her. She'd responded to his kisses, to his practised love-making. She, the modest maiden, the one who knew of his rakish past, should have put an end to it. The shame was all hers!

Then contrition hit her with a vengeance. She hadn't been thinking of her sister at all. Leighton only had to touch her and she forgot everything she held dear, including Marianne, her sister and the girl who was to marry him. He wasn't her man, he was her sister's, and she'd betrayed them both. She was being drawn into a quagmire of her own making, a dreadful web of deceit in which she was forced to pretend love for the viscount.

Pretend! She groaned out loud. She truly did love him, but she couldn't have him. Marianne, where are you? I need you. Then she became aware that both Leighton and his sister were staring at her.

Clarissa's mind dimly acknowledged the pair had been talking, but for the life of her, she couldn't recall what they had said. Surely Richard had mentioned something about business in the north?

'You're going away?' She turned tremulous eyes on Leighton, quite unable to decide whether she ought to be pleased to find him out of temptation's way, or to be sorry, in that she might never again meet him as a lover.

'I must, Marianne. I've urgent business to transact. I'm leaving this very morning, in a very few minutes. I came only to say my goodbyes.'

Since they all three knew he'd come to pour out his love and renew his offer of marriage, this seemed a very lame excuse. Clarissa, for her part, wondered if he'd conceived a disgust of her for returning his embrace with such ardour when they weren't even formally betrothed as yet. She felt the heat in his eyes on her and immediately realized it was no such thing. If Caroline left them alone then he'd reprise his scandalous behaviour without the slightest twinge of conscience. She blushed again, realizing she'd react just as passionately, and with as little sense of propriety.

Then why was he leaving so suddenly? She turned to Caroline, instinctively perceiving that she, too, was dismayed by this abrupt and inexplicable amendment to her brother's plans.

Having taken a formal leave, Richard was walked to the door by his sister, who very soon returned to quiz her future sister-in-law.

'What was that about? I thought you'd resolved all your differences. Indeed he swore to me he wished to renew his offer.'

'He did.' Clarissa was uncharacteristically quiet, wondering just what Richard really felt. She could see that Caroline had been taken as much by surprise as she by his sudden decision to leave.

'Then—'

'I accepted.' Clarissa's voice was cold. 'I can't tell you any more than that.' She blushed when she remembered what else she'd been offering. If they'd been alone? No, to think that way was madness. It was her sister he loved, and he'd be happy once she returned to him. He must love Marianne, for she couldn't deceive her own sister.

Caroline laughed at the play of emotions reflected in her future sister-in-law's face and decided she was truly in love with her brother. Perhaps Richard hadn't made himself clear.

'My dear,' she began, 'you may have no worries that Richard doesn't love you as truly as you love him. He might have entered the match for the convenience of having an heir to continue the line, but, depend on it, his feelings have changed. Once he took the trouble to really get to know you, love began to blossom in his heart. I swear I saw it the first time we met. Richard has never acted that way with a lady before, not even when I saw him with …' Her voice trailed off. Very likely Marianne had no idea of his entanglement with Lady Darcross, but if she did, she would hardly like to be reminded of the affair.

'Lady Darcross, you mean?' Clarissa felt a moment of illogical jealousy. Richard had loved before; indeed if the rector's description of him was true, had loved many times.

'You needn't concern yourself with that wretched woman, Marianne. Richard has never really been one for the ladies, and though he may have dallied with a ladybird from the opera on occasion, he's never behaved with the impropriety of many young men about Town. Lady Darcross flung out palpable lures to which he responded. The affair became the talk of Town, more because Richard had cut out Lord Dalwinton from her affections, than any violence of their own feelings. To tell the truth, the affair was over almost before it began. Richard soon saw through the lady's outward charms to the vile core within.'

'Dalwinton?' Clarissa's tone voiced her repugnance, and she shivered. She'd met him only briefly, but remembered the name from her sister's letters. 'He is the truly evil one.'

'They say he attempted to force a quarrel on Richard over the matter,' Caroline concurred, 'but talk of a duel came to nothing.'

'I should hope not.' Clarissa felt a qualm for her sister. She knew from Marianne's letters that Dalwinton had tried to force himself upon her, and immediately decided that act must have been aimed at wounding Richard, perhaps even to further the quarrel. No doubt Dalwinton was an expert with both gun and sword and would have favoured a duel with his rival. Had he gone further and kidnapped Marianne? She closed her eyes weakly and attempted to reassure herself. Sophie, though she might refuse to betray Marianne's hiding place, would never betray the girl herself. And her maidservant most surely knew where her sister was to be found.

'No, indeed. The very thought of it makes me sick,' returned Caroline, wondering just what was occupying her future sister-in-law's mind. She didn't seem over concerned about his connection with the Lady Darcross. Was it his dangerous dealings with Lord Dalwinton?

In fact, following Caroline's candid disclosures of her lover's past, Clarissa felt even more wretched in deceiving her friend, whom she'd already grown to love, knowing such a deed was almost as detestable as her behaviour to her beloved Richard. Neither of them could ever forgive her once they discovered her deception, and she was beginning to believe such an event must be inevitable unless Marianne returned to the fold immediately.

'Why not rejoice?' Caroline went on, seeking to charm

Clarissa out of her mopes. 'Richard must be happy in his future bride. You must be happy. I, too, for I've gained a sister whom I love as much as my brother.' She slid a comforting arm around her friend's waist, 'and I can't suppose that you didn't return firm evidence of his regard while you were alone.'

'You shouldn't have left us.'

'No, indeed, but I'll wager you both enjoyed the time you had together.' She laughed out loud when the blushes flared up again on Clarissa's face. 'Really Marianne, the way you leapt apart was a joy to watch, and nothing to blush over, I assure you.'

'I deceived him.'

'I doubt it.' Caroline didn't notice the change in Clarissa's demeanour immediately. 'Richard's more experienced than you'll ever know. He'd have noticed if you'd attempted to fake your passion.'

'I didn't …' Clarissa broke down in tears. 'I couldn't … Oh, I cannot go on with this deception.'

'Marianne?' Caroline stared at her charge in bewilderment.

'You'll hate me, but I must confess, Caroline.' Clarissa sat up straight and faced her erstwhile friend. 'I'm not Marianne. Not the girl Richard must love. He is truly betrothed to my sister.'

'What?'

Clarissa broke down again. The day had been too much for her. If only Richard hadn't given in to his romantic feelings and offered for her again. If only! No sense in asking such stupid questions of herself. She stared at Caroline's confused face and confessed the whole.

'I'm Marianne's twin, Clarissa,' she began. 'Marianne herself has disappeared, we know not where, but I took her place in an effort both to protect her name and to find her. Richard and yourself were innocent bystanders to the play, and I'm afraid the victims also.'

'You fell in love with him?'

'Yes.' Clarissa dropped her head and began to sob, amazed when Caroline slipped her arms around her shoulders to comfort her.

'You poor girl,' she murmured gently, and drew her down to her bosom. Poor Richard, too, she thought, and began to stroke the frantically sobbing girl's hair. He could be dreadfully proud and she dreaded to think how he'd take the news of his beloved's deceit.

CHAPTER THIRTEEN

A Secret is Unearthed

Clarissa lived through the next few days with a growing sense of foreboding. Caroline had kept her near for several hours following her confession, and appeared to accept the deception with every indication of complaisance, though she herself had been utterly distraught.

'Take care not to reveal the whole to Richard,' had been her friend's final instruction. 'I will undertake to soften the blow first.' She'd looked unusually serious, too.

Since Clarissa wasn't over confident in her ability to confess her sins to Richard in person, that was one piece of advice she had every intention of obeying to the letter. She shouldn't have admitted her guilt to Caroline either, and well she knew it. Marianne was relying on her to play a part, and she had an uneasy suspicion Richard would hear the whole from his sister as soon as he returned from wherever his singularly odd business had taken him.

Neither had the viscount's sister been sanguine in imagining he'd receive the news of his fiancé's deception lightly, Clarissa decided, having clearly recognized the dismay evident in her friend's expression. Caroline might have forgiven a green girl for the liberties she'd taken in playing the part of her sister, but no such reliance could be placed on Richard following in her footsteps. Just like his sister, she knew all too well his pride in the family honour. He'd even been willing to sacrifice his bachelor freedom to marry a girl he barely knew, merely because she was the *nonpareil* his consequence as head of the family deserved. His pride, and that of his entire family, would be dented beyond repair if the disgraceful history of her imposture reached the ears of the gossips.

Her sister, too, would be caught in the fall out. Not only would Marianne lose her chance at a titled husband, but perhaps any hope of a match at all, and her sister, as Clarissa well knew, could never be truly happy if she were forced to return to living a quiet existence in the country.

Her own situation was very different; she'd have to retire from society whether Leighton knew of their deception or not. Once Marianne returned to the fold, she herself must disappear forever. It would be one thing for Marianne to introduce a twin who looked so exactly like her into society when she was herself established, but quite another when that twin had already found the love of her life in the arms of her husband.

Clarissa began to regard Doctor Pym in the light of a saviour. He'd attempted a proposal on more than one occasion, and she knew she'd have to accept if he could be brought up to the mark again. She'd make him a good wife, she decided, never seek to put him to the blush, and they'd be happy. Well, she amended, with much more truthfulness, he'd be happy, for she'd never offer him any less than a good wife should.

Perhaps they could advance themselves as missionaries. To Africa, or even further continents, then abruptly stopped such self-indulgent dreaming. The rector wouldn't be at all comfortable with such a life; he wasn't a man destined to survive the rigours of such a calling, and nor could she, in all conscience, ask it of him. She would grow old instead, a spinster in company with Aunt Constance most likely.

There was no further news of Sophie either. Mr Markham had forbidden Clarissa to go out alone, and made it depressingly clear her replacement maid was specifically instructed to refuse to accompany her into any situation that was less than respectable. That being so, she was unlikely to catch even a glimpse of her erstwhile maidservant, who'd undoubtedly shun any thoughts of visiting more respectable areas for fear of being recognized.

It would be awkward, too, even if she were lucky enough to discover the girl, for she would then be obliged to give her new maid the slip before she could follow her. Not that such an event seemed likely, for all she kept her eyes open at every opportunity.

The business of society continued also. A ball, an assembly or two and an elegant card party filled up her evenings. Caroline, when she was present, sought her out with every indication of pleasure, pledging her friendship while steadfastly denying any knowledge of Leighton's whereabouts. Clarissa could only maintain a fashionable, but quite uncharacteristic sense of ennui. Without Richard at her side such entertainments could only bore her.

Leighton's return was unheralded by any of the portents of doom Clarissa had imagined. Edward brought news of his visit to her in the morning-room one afternoon when the Markhams were out. Aunt Eleanor was at her most favoured modiste and her Uncle John was visiting one of his clubs. None the less, for all the world knew, she was to be betrothed to the man and could hardly refuse to see him, even without her aunt and uncle to add their consequence. She raised her chin proudly and bade the footman show him in.

'Richard.' She stood stiff and still, wondering if he'd spoken to his sister before calling on her. If so this might be the last time she'd ever see him, and his visit mark the end of her sojourn in the capital.

'Forgive me, my darling. I haven't had a chance to change, having just ridden in, but your footman was good enough to brush me down.' He strode across the floor, and though none but the most elegant of dandies could have discovered the dirt on his 'Jean de Bry' riding coat or pale biscuit-coloured and skin-tight pantaloons, a muddy splash could be seen to have barely soiled the gleam of his buckskin boots. 'I couldn't wait to see you, dear one.'

'Oh.' Clarissa found herself swept into his embrace without ceremony, and before she could object, he was kissing her stupid.

'Clarissa,' he murmured into her ear. 'Clarissa, my darling.'

'No. Oh, no.' Though she couldn't help but return his ardent kisses, she knew she had to confess all before his sister did. Caroline's advice might have been sound, but Clarissa recognized she had to nerve herself to deliver the news. It was her responsibility.

'Please,' she cried out again, and tore her mouth away from his. 'Wait, only wait.' She held her hands to her face when she realized how he was addressing her. 'What did you call me?' she quavered.

'Why, by your name, of course,' he returned with a laugh. Then he kissed her soundly before she could object. 'Clarissa,' he breathed at last. 'I can think of any no other name that would suit you half so well, nor me either.'

'You have seen your sister, then?'

'What! Does she know also? That's famous. I thought we'd have to keep it as our secret.'

'She wasn't sure …' Clarissa voice tailed off. 'How did you know?'

'By your own goosish behaviour,' he returned. 'My dear Clarissa, whatever possessed you to attempt such a deception?'

'My sister had disappeared.' She didn't attempt to tell him the story in full. He hadn't as yet answered her own question. 'You might have suspected me when you renewed your offer, but you said nothing to me, nor did you realize who I was, or my name.'

'I'm sorry, Clarissa, my love. I could say nothing while I had only the vaguest of suspicions in my mind. I thought at first you were indeed Marianne, for how could I have suspected your twin to be so exactly alike. Only you're not alike. You're so much more gentle, more loving.' He paused for a moment of tender regard. 'You love me in a way your sister never could. We're soul-mates, something Marianne, for all her virtues, never could be. She and I would have entered into a civil contract, a marriage of pure convenience, providing her with the noble marriage she craved and me with a pretty plaything.'

'Where did you go?' Clarissa stared at him intently. She didn't like to think of Richard toying with a pretty plaything, even if it was her sister.

'I made a visit to your Aunt Constance.'

'My Aunt Constance?'

'A most worthy woman,' he conceded. 'She was surprised to see me and even more astonished when I laid the parts of my puzzle before her. I thought at first that Marianne's illness might have changed her character, but your aunt soon disabused me of that notion. Once she learned I was irretrievably in love with you, she told me the whole, including the history of your sister's mysterious disappearance. Now, Clarissa, we may be married in truth.'

'No,' she told him distractedly. 'It is worse than ever. How can I steal my own sister's future husband?' She gasped at the sudden realization. 'As my mother stole Eleanor's.'

'Eleanor?'

'Aunt Eleanor, Mrs Markham. Her betrothed ran off with my mother when Marianne and I were but babes in arms. Aunt Constance has taken her place in our hearts ever since, but you must surely see that I can never undertake such a scandalous act. My reputation and the reputation of the Leighton family would be ruined forever.'

'I cannot be expected to marry your sister,' he told her shortly, 'when it's you I love.'

'It would be wicked beyond measure to cast her off. Your betrothal is such a poorly kept secret that every jokester in society would make her the butt of his wit, and it would be so much the worse if her own sister were to take her place. Neither would the Leighton family's standing in society be improved by such an ill-considered action and, as for me,' – Clarissa knew exactly what the quizzes would say – 'I should be labelled as my mother's true born daughter to serve Marianne in such an infamous manner.'

'There must be something we could do.' Richard shook his head in desperation. 'No formal notification of the betrothal has yet been given.'

'I don't see how,' Clarissa replied bitterly, 'you could publicly renounce your claim to her hand, and immediately take up with me in her place without subjecting us all to the tender mercies of the ton.'

'I won't give you up,' he swore in return. 'Even if we have to leave the country.'

Clarissa knew Richard's plea for the nonsense it was, and though she secretly exulted in the knowledge that it was his love for her that made him utter it, she also knew that any such plan was doomed from the start. Leighton was the head of his family. His life, his estates, everything he held dear was situated in England. She couldn't allow him to give up everything for her. Nor could she allow herself to steal her sister's future husband!

'I believe I must be taken ill again,' she told him. 'I'll return to the countryside until Marianne reappears.' The future began to look bleak to her; forced to leave the pleasures of London and the man she loved.

'No,' he told her firmly. 'The scandal will only loom so much the larger if it were ever discovered that not one, but two sisters have disappeared. You must remain at my side while we institute a search for Marianne. The two of us working together will surely discover her directly.'

Clarissa considered the compromise and nodded her acceptance. Leighton had bravely accepted the situation, as she must herself. They'd be friends, of course, but nothing more. A bleak future awaited her, and secretly she knew she'd have to travel abroad herself. Even retirement to the country could never reconcile her to their parting.

A bleak future indeed!

CHAPTER FOURTEEN

At Chatsbury's Masque

Despite her misgivings, Clarissa knew she must continue to enjoy all that society could offer. Indeed, she could hardly refuse to attend those parties her aunt decided were eligible. At first she thought that such entertainments would be drained of all pleasure for her, but although she continued to be haunted by Marianne's absence, she soon realized how easily her treacherous heart could leap when Lord Leighton entered the room.

The latest of these entertainments was to take the form of a masque, a very select and private affair arranged by Lord Chatsbury. Since Clarissa had contrived since revealing her deception to Leighton, to meet him only in the most public of places, she'd eyed the hastily arranged party with some misgivings. Chatsbury and Leighton were bosom buddies and she couldn't doubt they'd conspired to arrange the sudden engagement between them. Aunt Eleanor, however, held no such doubts: Chatsbury was a most eligible host and she had no intention of disappointing him by refusing to attend.

Clarissa consoled herself by deciding that, despite the entertainment being labelled a select party, there would be considerable numbers attending, and she could easily keep

Richard at arm's length. The truth was she didn't trust herself to maintain the proprieties if she were left alone with him; nor him, if he were alone with her. Nevertheless, she was determined not to let her fears stop herself enjoying the event, never having attended a masque before.

Her friend, Emily, had attended one only a week since, at Vauxhall. It was a public event, and one where Aunt Eleanor, ever the high stickler, had refused her consent for Clarissa to join her. From all she'd said, it seemed that Emily had enjoyed the spectacle immensely, though even that pert miss had to admit the jostling crowds spoiled some of her pleasure. That some of the more vulgar elements, emboldened by the anonymity endowed by their masks, should have indulged in rather less than virtuous behaviour, hadn't fazed her one bit. Indeed, she'd thoroughly enjoyed the spectacle, and following the common practice of removing their masks at midnight, had confessed to her delight in finding several other likewise respectable acquaintances in the booths alongside the central walkway at the venue.

Cheered by a reverie of elegant and colourful lanterns lighting the gardens of the Chatsbury's town mansion and the spectacular fireworks to follow, Clarissa was only too pleased to let her new maid dress her for the occasion.

Her hair had been coiffured with a parting in the centre and arranged into full ringlets on either side of her face, speared with ribbons to match her dress. This was cut low on the bodice with a fashionable high waist and made of silk gauze, in a pale jonquil, with an under-dress of satin. The long, full sleeves were frilled at the wrist, and bust and shoulders emphasized by skilfully applied bands of silk. A skein of pale, iridescent pearls with matching ear-drops and low-heeled sandals with ankle ties and three strips across the vamp completed her outfit, apart from the mask. This was an all concealing, full face mask, painted in fantastical designs and colours to enhance her gown, its facets cunningly designed to reflect the light in stunning rainbows while effectively concealing her features.

The Markhams and their niece drove to the party in their barouche, a little old-fashioned by the standard of the times, but owning a certain elegance which Uncle John set great store by. To Clarissa's relief, the masque was as well attended as she'd expected and, hidden behind the protection of her mask, she hoped to delay, if not circumvent, any meeting with Lord Leighton – a fruitless aspiration, as she soon found out for herself.

Clarissa quickly found herself separated from her relatives, but didn't mind that in the least. A party of young revellers danced by on their way to the gardens, but though she recognized Emily amongst them, she disregarded all their pleas to join them. The gravest dangers would lie in a garden Leighton surely knew like the back of his hand.

'Clarissa, my dear.' Caroline greeted her unexpectedly. 'You look absolutely ravishing. And your mask is so beautiful, I hardly recognized you.' Her own mask barely covered her eyes and was in addition worn so askew as to render it easy to identify her.

'I saw you arrive with the Markhams,' she went on artlessly. 'Their barouche is very distinctive and Sir Roger and I were in line a few carriages behind you.' Then she explained her skill at recognizing her young friend despite the all enveloping mask. 'Roger made straight for the card room, leaving me without an escort. I hope you don't mind me attaching myself to you.'

'Of course not,' Clarissa assured her. She looked around carefully and asked the question with a nonchalance she certainly didn't feel. 'Is Richard here? Or is he coming later?'

'Have you not seen him yet? He's tricked out in a black lacquer mask it's hard to miss.'

Clarissa hadn't noticed it as yet, but when she stared over her friend's shoulder, she saw the very image of such a mask approaching.

'Come,' she told Caroline at once. 'Let's go and see the garden. I hear Chatsbury's furnished a very fine lantern show, and doubtless Richard's already made his way out there.' She slipped an arm under Caroline's and began to lead her outside, ruthlessly stemming any mutinous reaction from her friend by talking herself blue in the face. 'I'm really looking forward to watching the fireworks,' she started to prattle, 'but I dare say they won't start until midnight.'

'So I'm informed.' Lord Leighton spoke more gravely than his usual fashion, but there was no doubt as to his person. The mask was, as Caroline had foretold, a plain, black affair that covered most his face. He turned to his sister when they entered the gardens together. 'You will excuse us, I'm sure, Caro. Clarissa and I have much to discuss.'

It was the use of her own name that gave Clarissa pause. It made them somehow more intimate, alone together, although they were still in the midst of a crowd. Richard took her arm and she consented to be drawn away from the safe ground next to his sister. Not that he ever had any intention of letting me escape, she reflected warily.

'Please, Richard,' she made the attempt in form, 'we cannot trust ourselves alone for the sake of our families.'

'Fustian.' Richard's reply was as short as it was inelegant. He continued to hustle her through the garden, gradually drawing her away from the more populated parts, down a lonely, unlit path which led to God alone knew where. Not quite true, for Richard also evidently knew the way, and no doubt the gardeners did too, though they'd be nowhere close while the party continued.

'We'll be betrothed within a week.' Richard brought their progress to a halt in the shelter of a stone circle in the darkest part of the garden. The lanterns still flared eerily in the distance and Clarissa could see his face clearly when he deftly removed his mask.

'We cannot let it go ahead, Richard.' She made her plea again. 'Aunt Eleanor must postpone the event.' She couldn't bear the thought of hurting Marianne, nor yet of distressing Leighton. But either way she'd wound one of them, and in any event she'd hurt herself.

'That would please the gossips,' he laughed, 'and Mrs Markham too, I suspect.' His voice was serious. 'You cannot put off a ball for no apparent reason, and neither can you put off a betrothal that most of the ton already suppose to be a done thing. No, Clarissa, you must realize the engagement will go ahead whether you like it or not.' He tucked a gentle finger under her chin and raised her face to his own, impatiently stripping away her enveloping mask. 'I intend a betrothal, dear one, and I expect our wedding to follow swiftly on its heels. A marriage between you and I, Clarissa. A loving union between us, not an attempt to foist a deception on my friends and family, to say nothing of your own.'

His lips descended and claimed her soft mouth for his own. The troubles of the world, even her sister's sad plight, seemed to pale before the passion he unleashed, and Clarissa found herself lost in his arms once more. She clung to him breathlessly, returning his embrace with a fervour that shook her slim form like the wind through fields of corn.

'A pretty picture, to be sure.' The very words, insultingly drawled, seemed to match the sneer on Lord Dalwinton's face.

He held up one hand and stared at it as though to inspect the cut of his nails, 'but which sister is it you're kissing, I wonder?'

Clarissa, who'd instinctively shrunk behind Leighton at the man's appearance, stepped forward ready for battle. 'You should already know the answer to that impertinent question, sir. You're the so-called gentleman who tried to force his attentions on me when you thought I had no one to protect me. Lord Leighton, I beg to inform you, owns the grace to wait until he finds a maiden willing to accept his kisses.'

Leighton caught hold of her and drew her back, slipping his arm protectively around her shoulders, while his eyes continued to bore into the nobleman with chilling purpose.

'You must already know, Dalwinton, that Miss Meredew and I are to be formally betrothed within the week.'

'Indeed.' Lord Dalwinton executed a graceful bow in their direction. 'I confess I had heard something of the sort, but I can only assume you have no preference for which sister.'

'He had better, sir.' Clarissa stormed back into the attack. 'And I can only assume you've forgotten you're a gentleman when you bandy these ridiculous accusations about.' She glared at him angrily, totally unaware her fingers had hooked into vicious claws. The gentle sister had turned into the very image of a fierce lioness, risking all to defend her loved one.

'Please,' Dalwinton's smile failed to reach his eyes and his words lacked any suggestion of true contrition, but it was plain he was shaken by the violence with which Clarissa had refuted the suggestions. 'I declare I feel nothing but admiration for the pair of you.'

'Then I beg you won't embarrass the lady by spreading ugly rumours,' Leighton followed up, in a voice so urbane it sounded almost menacing. 'Particularly when they're so palpably false.'

'Quite so.' Dalwinton was bested and so he knew. He executed another bow towards Clarissa's stormy figure. 'I must leave you lovers alone, I fear, but have a care. These gardens are not so private as they look.'

The pair watched him anxiously while he minced away, waiting until he disappeared into the gloom before they spoke again.

'Does he really know the truth about my deception?' Clarissa posed the question that was on both their minds.

'That he suspects you're not Marianne is the only inference I can make. For what reason I can't tell.' Leighton thought long and hard before he continued, 'I can only assume he has some knowledge of Marianne's disappearance denied the remainder of the ton. Nevertheless, with the pair of you alike as two peas in a pod, he still can't be sure of his facts, and was looking to startle us into providing irrefutable proof. Luckily for us, he has no such evidence, for he'd happily broadcast the news to all society our quarrel runs so deep.'

'Can he be holding Marianne himself?'

'No.' Leighton shook his head decisively. 'You saw the answer to that in his words. He only suspects you're not her, may not even know she has a twin. If he had her imprisoned, then he'd have the proof to hand, though he could hardly dare to use it.' He stared at the girl with a strangely menacing light in his eyes. 'What's this about him attempting to kiss you?'

'Not myself, but Marianne,' she corrected. 'She wrote of his attempt in one of her letters. Someone, an acquaintance of hers, came to her rescue and struck him down. I dare say he'd like to be revenged for that also.'

'Then he's doubly dangerous,' decided Leighton. 'We already know he suspects your role and that he's out for revenge. That being so we can assume he will mount his own search for your sister, or perhaps he's already started.' The viscount's brows knitted in thought. 'He knows more of this story than we give him credit for,' he decided. 'He cannot have detected your impersonation by his own deductions; he knows neither you nor Marianne intimately enough to pierce your disguise. That being so, he must have other evidence to go on. Your maid perhaps, or could he have seen your sister's note?'

'No,' Clarissa returned confidently. 'My aunt and uncle keep it locked away and, whatever her faults, I'm convinced Sophie is too devoted to my sister to betray her. Even to me.'

'No use floundering in the dark,' decided Leighton wearily. 'He must have some basis for his suspicions, but it's all the same to us whatever it may be. We must accelerate our own search.'

'What if he finds her first?'

'Forewarned is forearmed.' Leighton tucked her hand under his arm and began to stroll back towards the lighted area. 'We'll keep our eyes on Lord Dalwinton and in the meantime, you may permit me to take you riding in my curricle. For the benefit of the curious, there's a good deal of London you still haven't seen. Can you arrange for your groom to be temporarily transferred to my staff? We may need his help in our quest, and it'll save a lot of awkward questions if he's seen to be employed as my tiger.'

'I'll speak to Uncle John at breakfast tomorrow morning. I can't think he'll have any objection, but old Mr Harricot, who manages the stables, might not like the idea quite so well; Tom's his son, an only child I believe.'

'Then he'll be all the more pleased for the lad's unexpected advancement. Taken on as tiger to a nobleman! It could be the making of him. What sort of father wouldn't be celebrating his promotion?'

'You'll drive me out tomorrow?'

'If you're free.' Leighton eyed her with glee in his eyes. 'I suggest we meet up at my sister's residence. Nothing for the gossips to dwell on there. Will late morning suit you?'

Clarissa bit her lip. She vividly remembered the last time they'd met at Caroline's house. Not that there was anything in that for her to dwell on either. She wouldn't allow him to continue his deplorable practice of making love to her every time he met her. Nor would she allow Caroline to leave them alone. Best not to present him with temptation.

'I'll be there,' she confirmed sweetly.

'You can tell me everything you know about Marianne's disappearance once we're private. Now, we must dance, it wouldn't be seemly to slip away again tonight. Not until we're formally betrothed.' He slipped her mask back on and led her back into the conservatory where a number of guests were already gathering in a set for a country dance.

CHAPTER FIFTEEN

The Search for Marianne

Next morning Clarissa went down to breakfast early. It was a convenient time for her to catch her uncle, for Mr Markham was an early riser by society standards, and though he was usually still busy at the table when she appeared, this could be by no means relied upon. They'd be alone too, for Aunt Eleanor rarely left her boudoir before the breakfast dishes had been cleared.

'Uncle John.' She started on her mission after exchanging the usual bland inanities about the weather and the state of the nation.

'Yes, my dear.' John Markham was fond of his niece and quite ready to indulge her. Clarissa, he considered, had far greater consequence than the more volatile Marianne, and moreover, he assured himself, she wouldn't be forever running off and leaving them to the mercy of society gossips.

He didn't altogether approve of the scheme his wife had presented to him as a *fait accompli* either. In his opinion Clarissa should have been looking for a husband of her own, and not running around deceiving her sister's beau. However, he fully realized the advantages of the deception, both to Marianne and themselves, and had reluctantly been talked around to back the plan. Then again, since Clarissa had already been seen, if only by the servants, he'd been left with little option.

'Richard ... Lord Leighton has asked me to enquire if you'd lend him young Tom for a period. He needs him as tiger for his carriage.'

'I thought you'd installed him as your groom, my dear?' Clarissa didn't like the way her uncle was looking at her. She'd already decided he wasn't a man who could be easily fooled, but neither could she admit the truth. If he discovered Leighton knew of the deception he was quite capable of packing her back off to the countryside.

'So I had, but Leighton's need is the greater. He's engaged to show me the sights and must have a groom on hand to maintain the proprieties.' Even Clarissa couldn't explain how she was able to lie so fluently under his scrutiny without putting herself to the blush.

'I wonder what happened to Leighton's man? Been with him for years, I understand.' Mr Markham seemed to accept the situation at face value. 'Do as you think fit, my dear. It'll do no harm to keep Leighton sweet with the betrothal so close at hand.'

'Thank you.' Clarissa smiled sweetly. 'I have hopes for Marianne to take her place in time for the ball. She's never been one to miss a party.'

'It would be embarrassing for us all if she isn't,' Mr Markham reminded her. 'You will hardly like to take her place at such a ceremony.'

'No, indeed not.' Clarissa's agreement was so heart-felt that her uncle looked up startled.

'Has he been pressing you too far, my dear?' he asked.

'Oh no. You mustn't think I repine.' She unblushingly

returned a negative answer and attempted to reassure him. 'Leighton always acts the complete gentleman in my company.'

'Then he's a damned fool.' Mr Markham speared her with a penetrating glare and went off on a sudden tangent that caught her by surprise. 'You've fallen in love with him, haven't you, lass?'

'Yes,' she admitted, hanging her head low.

'Does he know it?'

'I believe so, Uncle. That is …' Clarissa had conceived the intention of informing her uncle that she and Leighton never talked of their love, but decided that was one lie of which she would never convince him.

'We should not have entered on this deception,' he decided forlornly. 'My wife's bacon-brained ideas have a way of straying awry, but I blame myself more than anyone.' He regarded her fondly. 'You have more to lose than anyone if Marianne returns.'

'I sincerely hope she does, Uncle.'

'Aye, lass. I know you do.' Mr Markham nodded kindly. 'But you'd lose Leighton, if ever she did.'

'She's my sister,' she cried. 'I could never steal him from her. Even if …' She dropped her head when her shuddering voice ground to a halt, as near to tears as she'd ever been.

'He knows, doesn't he?'

Clarissa stared at her uncle in dismay. 'Knows what?' The dissemblance was poor as she very well knew.

'Will he take Marianne?'

Clarissa hesitated a little too long. 'He must,' she confirmed.

'We're all in the suds if he doesn't.' Mr Markham seemed to age before her eyes. 'I take it you're seeing him this morning.'

'I'm promised to Lady Burnett, his sister,' she confirmed,

leaving out the fact that she, too, knew of their deception. Her uncle's peace was cut up enough already. 'He usually waits on her in the morning.'

'Take him yourself, if you can,' he advised kindly. 'Your sister doesn't deserve such devotion.' He stood up from the table abruptly. 'I have some correspondence to deal with.'

Less than an hour later Clarissa found herself in the Markhams' carriage on its journey to Lady Burnett's residence. Tom clung to the back of the vehicle, a canvas hold-all containing his baggage strapped to the top, while his father drove, usurping the coachman's place to bid a farewell to his son.

She bestowed a rail on the lad when they arrived and begged him to help all he could in finding her sister, then left him to his father, in whose breast, she was sure, pride was inextricably mixed with the sorrow of parting.

Caroline's butler showed her into the morning-room where Caroline waited with her brother.

'I have brought Tom,' she told him when he advanced on her. Then hissed in a quiet, sibilant tone, designed to be heard by him alone, 'No, we must not. Your sister—' The plea was ruthlessly thrust aside and a leisurely kiss pressed on her cheek, and that only because she turned her lips away.

'I think I'd better leave you.' Clarissa found to her horror that Caroline was already heading for the door.

'No,' she cried.

'Yes.' Richard took her arm and led her to a seat on the far side of the room. 'Caroline cannot be further implicated in our plots. Come, sit down, and I promise to behave.' He looked at her disbelieving face with a grave intensity and added a disturbing rider. 'For the present.'

'Marianne.' Clarissa reminded him of their purpose.

'Tell me the whole,' he requested. 'Leave nothing out, however distasteful. I have to know what we're dealing with.'

Clarissa obediently did as he told her, happy to discover that he largely agreed with her own conclusions. Despite her long absence it seemed to him, as to her, that Marianne was merely in hiding of her own accord, and meant to return to the bosom of her family in time.

Why did she leave? That question was germane only in that it might give a clue to her present whereabouts. As for its answer, Leighton had as little idea as Clarissa, though he could apply some reasoned argument. Her decision must have been unexpected and sudden, for she'd evidently been forced to implicate her maid at the last moment, if only to supply her with the clothing she'd require. No well-planned flight to the border, then. Equally likely that she would have remained in the neighbourhood of the park where she was last seen; with her own carriage so close by it would make no sense to hire another if she found it necessary to undertake a further journey. Since his logic took him no further than Clarissa had already related, he dismissed this line of reasoning and started afresh.

'Why was Marianne in such a neighbourhood?' he asked. The question was rhetoric and Clarissa knew it as well as he. 'From what you say, it was a respectable part of town, but not a place where anyone of any consequence would live. She could not have found a friend living there.'

'She told Aunt Eleanor she was going to the Emporium.'

'You say there was no sign of any shops, either,' mused Leighton.

'She could have been meeting someone.' Clarissa blushed, well aware that Leighton would consider his future wife had no right to be meeting anyone in secret, especially in such an out of the way place.

'An assignation, in fact,' he returned coolly, taking in Clarissa's embarrassment. 'Have you been keeping something from me?'

'No,' she floundered. 'Well, nothing you couldn't have decided for yourself.' She continued to blush for her sister's notions of propriety. 'As I've already told you she mentioned a lad named Stephen in her letters. I thought she might perhaps have been meeting him.'

'Yes,' he nodded calmly. 'That theory would certainly fit the facts as we know them. Did no one suspect?'

'Rumours of her elopement were running rife when I first came to London,' admitted the girl. 'My appearance scotched them before they could damage her reputation, but I never did believe them, and nor should you. She'd have brought her baggage along with her, if that were her plan, and very likely taken her maid too. Marianne is no giddy girl.'

'Is there anything else I should know?' Leighton raised his eyebrows in mute question. 'Lord Dalwinton, for example?'

'Dalwinton? I can't believe she would stoop to meeting him in secret. For all he's received in society, he's no better than the most ramshackle of rakes.' Clarissa dismissed the idea of a tryst with such a man. 'Why, if Marianne's letters are to be believed, she positively disliked the man.'

'If he suspects you're not Marianne,' Leighton prompted, 'then he must have some reason for doing so. I cannot believe he plays no part in this whole imbroglio.'

'Perhaps he intended to blackmail her.' A pure guess, based on the reading of the most trashy romantic novels. Clarissa had no great knowledge of the blackmailer's art, but she doubted whether any of Marianne's escapades would result in that much notoriety.

'No, not blackmail,' Leighton replied. 'Dalwinton has no

need of money; his estates are amongst the richest in the country. Besides, if Marianne had laid herself open to anything of that kind, he'd have used the information gained to torment me. The whole of society knew we were about to be betrothed, and he has scores to settle.'

'Then we come, as always, to the same answer,' Clarissa confirmed wearily. 'Marianne made an appointment to meet a mysterious person in a respectable, but not particularly refined part of the city, and promptly disappeared for no reason we can discover.'

'Not quite so,' Leighton reminded her. 'We have a meeting place, and we have suspects, even if we can't decide on their motives.' He held up his hand when Clarissa opened her mouth to speak. 'We also have Marianne's written word that she intends to return. That suggests that neither of our suspects has her held against her will.' He thought for a moment longer before laying out his plans. 'It'll be interesting to find out if Dalwinton knows where to prosecute his search, if indeed he does intend to institute an investigation of his own. I will also undertake to find the lad you mentioned. Stephen, wasn't it?'

'He was an army officer; on leave from the Continent, I believe.' Clarissa stared at her lover. 'How can you trace him?'

'I have some contacts at Horse Guards who might be useful.' He shrugged off the question. 'But in the meantime, Tom can guide me to the scene. I've not yet seen the park.'

'What about me?'

'You have a luncheon appointment with my sister.'

And with that Clarissa had to be satisfied.

Next morning Richard called on Clarissa early and, although she was still at breakfast, she immediately rose from the table to go to him. To her surprise Aunt Eleanor was there before her.

'I've been telling your aunt,' he told her mysteriously, 'that my sister urgently begs your company.'

The suppressed excitement in his voice convinced her there was more to be said and, were it not for her aunt's inhibiting presence, she would have begged him to tell her immediately.

'I'm sure you won't disappoint her,' he continued urbanely, but with such a look in his eye that Clarissa could guess the matter was urgent.

'Of course not,' she agreed, ruefully surveying her morning dress and deciding it wasn't suitable for a visit to such a fashionable lady, 'but first I must change. I don't doubt Aunt Eleanor will entertain you in the meantime.'

'Don't be too long, Tom's walking the horses,' Leighton warned her and bowed politely to her aunt, refusing any attempt to offer him sustenance. 'I must wait with him, ma'am.'

Leighton was all too obviously in a hurry and Clarissa wasted no more time than it took to snatch up a warm pelisse and reticule before she set off for the door. Her gown would have to do after all.

Aunt Eleanor had other ideas.

'Clarissa,' she scolded impatiently, too over-set to consider one of the servants might overhear her using the girl's true name. 'You cannot go driving alone with a single gentleman under such sudden circumstances, even if you are as good as betrothed. In such a rush too. You've only just emerged from breakfast. What would anyone think of you?'

'Caroline has need of me, Aunt.' What could Clarissa care of her reputation when it was obvious to her that Richard had a lead on Marianne's disappearance. 'I'll be back directly,' and she slipped through the door.

'Good girl,' Richard told her, while he handed her on to the vehicle. 'I haven't heard the whole myself as yet, but I can give you the gist, and my groom will update us both once we reach Caroline's.' Leaping athletically to the seat beside her, he took up the reins and began to tool the sporting carriage down the streets at a spanking pace.

'Teddy has been with me for several years and I'd trust him with my life. Indeed, I did so while he was my batman in the Peninsula. He's now my personal groom and is normally found playing tiger on my curricle.' He took a glance behind where Tom had usurped his fiercely loyal servant's place. 'I set him on to watch Dalwinton in case the old roué tried out any of his tricks.'

'Am I to assume he did?'

'Dalwinton led him directly to the very same part of the city as you described and Tom showed me.' His voice betrayed the excitement in his breast. 'It cannot any longer be doubted that Dalwinton has more knowledge than mere gossip to go on.' He held up one long, elegant finger to further capture her interest. 'Moreover,' he told her, 'Dalwinton's servant was sent chasing after a girl matching Sophie's description, who ran off to escape him.'

'Did she evade him?'

'She did, but you'll hear the whole from Teddy.'

'Good morning to you, miss.' Teddy greeted her politely when he was shown into Caroline's morning-room. Once again she'd obligingly given it up to their sole use.

Anxious to hear the entire story, Leighton cut through the preliminary obsequies with a request for his groom to 'cut wheedle.'

'Aye, sir. As you know I followed Lord Dalwinton to the same park as young Tom showed us earlier in the day. He dismounted from his carriage and, after looking about, began to stroll down one of the paths, the same route as Tom said the young lady took.' He paused slightly and coughed delicately, 'By which I mean your sister, begging your pardon, miss. Another cove, a manservant from the look of him, followed a pace or two behind.

'All of a sudden he raised his stick and pointed out a girl on the far side of the green. Pretty young thing she was, carrying a small bundle, and must have seen them as soon as they saw her, for she went off like a hare. Dalwinton's servant ran off after her, but she gave him the slip easy. Knew the back doubles like a native, she did. Don't slip my leash so easy, though. I was born in the stews and knows the streets as well as her.

'I thought she might not suspicion me at first, but she was cunning like. Took me right to the heart of the stews; like a rabbit warren it was. Then, when we entered the market I had to follow close in case she slipped out of sight in the crowds, like she wanted to. This big codger, he started to suspicion I was chasing her for no good. Right bully boy, he was, an' I reckon she set him on to me. No good to argue, but by the time I'd won free, the girl had disappeared.'

'Damnation.' Leighton gave vent to his feelings, but Clarissa, who vividly remembered suffering much the same experiences when she'd chased the girl herself, was apt to be kinder.

'I did get hold of this, gov.' Teddy continued his story, and handed over a bloodstained scarf.

'Marianne's. It was one of her favourites.' Clarissa turned quite pale when the groom exhibited the gory article.

'Old blood,' stated Leighton, examining the scarf in some detail. 'It must have dried up weeks since.' Then he attempted to calm his love's fears. 'A little blood goes a long way and it may not even be Marianne's.'

'No.' Clarissa was uncharacteristically quiet. 'But for all that someone was hurt and it wasn't Sophie.' Perhaps they had it wrong. Was Marianne being held against her will? Perhaps she was hurt, but why then wouldn't she return. Not dead, or Sophie wouldn't still be visiting her. 'Has she been kidnapped?' She turned her eyes on Richard.

'I don't know,' he told her gently, 'but I intend to set a watch on the neighbourhood myself. Teddy stayed out all night so he must be allowed to rest now.'

'Oh Teddy.' To the embarrassed groom's scarlet-faced amazement, Clarissa caught hold of one of his filthy hands and pressed it to her lips. 'Thank you, Teddy. You don't know how worried I've been for my sister's safety. She has a true friend in you.' She turned to Leighton and announced her own intentions. 'I'll accompany you, Richard. You may have need of me.'

'No.' He was firm on the point. 'Teddy has lent me suitably dirt-soiled work clothes to blend in with my surroundings. You'd stick out like a sore thumb.'

'I must insist.' Clarissa's voice had an edge of unwavering resolution he'd never heard before. 'I have a gown in my room, suitable only for the garden. Let me remind you too, that Sophie is hardly likely to open up to you even if you should catch her. Under such circumstances she may, however, speak more frankly to me.'

'When I find that silly girl, she'll give me the information I want.' Leighton, looking unusually leonine, was sure of his methods, though he had to admit that Clarissa's presence might smooth the way.

'We would also attract far less attention as a couple.' Clarissa heard the hesitation in his voice and pressed her advantage. 'If Marianne is found to be injured and abed, it will make things easier for you if her sister is available to nurse her.'

'No.'

'Then I'll make my own way there.'

It was a clincher and Leighton had to admit it. He conceded, justifying the decision by telling himself he could hardly lock her up, and furthermore, there was no risk of injury. Besides, in all likelihood they'd have to wait around for hours, during which time he could tease the girl to his heart's content.

'There's no time to drive you home,' he told her shortly. 'I'll instruct Caroline to requisition some old clothes from her maids. I dare say at least one of them is close enough to your size.'

Thus it was that less than an hour later, as disreputable couple as ever they'd hoped was to be found strolling in the park. Teddy's work clothes, a size too small for the viscount, were as dirty and greasy as Clarissa had expected, and her own, borrowed surreptitiously from the Cook's oldest daughter, were quite the shabbiest she'd ever worn.

However, though they waited for most of the day, they were unable to discover any trace of Sophie, or anyone else they knew.

'She must have been frightened off,' Leighton told Clarissa grimly, 'or she may not visit every day.'

'There's foul play involved,' returned the girl with a worried frown. 'Witness the blood on her scarf. That Dalwinton should be searching for her puts him under suspicion. Perhaps she remains in hiding from him.'

'That would explain Sophie running on sight of him yesterday,' admitted Leighton, 'but where would Marianne hide? She'd be safer from his attentions with the Markhams.'

'How about Lady Darcross? Jealousy may have caused her to imprison my sister. She knows Dalwinton well, I hear, and may have mentioned something to him that aroused his suspicions.'

'If you're referring to my recent amours, Lady Darcross's jealous rages are well known,' replied Leighton, 'but seldom go beyond throwing whatever article is handiest at her latest lover. My casting her off is unlikely to have caused a lasting fit, when she was seen in the company of a fine dandy the very next day.

'In any case, simply to abduct the girl makes no sense. If she did it to revenge herself on me, then she would need to flaunt the crime in my face and, by doing so, incriminate herself.'

'Then we're thwarted yet again.'

CHAPTER SIXTEEN

Found and Lost

Three days later they still had no additional clues, though Teddy continued to haunt the places he'd spotted Sophie, eating and sleeping in the roughest of conditions. Either the maid had discontinued her surreptitious visits to her mistress, or she was too fly to be caught again.

Leighton met him at least once every day and carried back his dispatches to Clarissa, who waited on his report with baited breath. The pair of them continued with their own pleasures most mornings, pretending to visit the sights, but in fact to keep the park under surveillance, though they never again bothered to don their rough disguises. Teddy, with all the advantages of his upbringing in the stews, might attempt to pursue her if he were fortunate enough to catch a glimpse of the girl, but they could never hope for success in such a venture. They could only aspire to snatch the girl if she was imprudent enough to come to close quarters. Unknown to Clarissa, Leighton, anxious to conclude the ugly deception, continued his watch into the afternoons as well.

Thus it was all the more surprising when the lucky break came not to Leighton, or his groom, but to Clarissa herself.

She had been used to spending her afternoons in the company of Caroline, with whom she'd forged a close friendship. On that day, the two fashionable ladies, accompanied by Caroline's maid and a young footman to carry the parcels, had repaired to the Emporium at the corner of Bridge Street to undertake the purchase of sufficient ribbons and bows to refurbish some of her ladyship's hats. The pile of parcels carried by Lady Burnett's footman bore mute witness to the success of their shopping, and they were returning to her carriage congratulating each other, when a lad, little older than Clarissa herself, appeared out of nowhere.

'Marianne!' Accustomed by now to reacting to her sister's name, Clarissa turned to regard the youngster quizzically, and immediately recognized he was older than she'd first speculated. Taller too, though that may have been due to the straightness in the way he held himself, a military man perhaps. He had an air of command to him, though it was currently overborne by the suspicion in his breast that he'd made a mistake. If he was indeed in the military, then his manners indicated it was as an officer, though he wore no uniform. Bought out perhaps; many young men of her acquaintance had done as much with the end of the wars against the French. Pale-faced, looked as though he'd recently been ill.

'Marianne, is it you?' He tried again, less sure of himself, but staring at Clarissa's face as though mesmerized.

'Yes.' Clarissa was sure she hadn't met the youth before, although he plainly knew her sister. No more than a slight acquaintance, or Marianne would have written of him.

'I beg your pardon, ma'am.' The lad held himself straighter than ever, and bowed slightly before he turned away.

'No, sir. I am indeed Marianne. You must forgive me for not recognizing you.' She risked a glance at Caroline who gave the slightest of nods to show she, too, had failed to identify him.

'Not the lady I know, however.' His embarrassment was betrayed by the flush on his face. 'Though you bear an astonishing likeness.'

'Stephen,' Clarissa ejaculated. The only astonishing likeness she bore was to her sister, and the only name she could associate with her sister's disappearance was that of the unknown lad who had himself vanished also. Though not, apparently, back to his regiment on the Continent.

'Ma'am.'

She was right. He didn't attempt to deny it, but even if he had, she'd already seen the answer in his eyes. He was astonished that she recognized him, more puzzled than she, for Clarissa held by far the greater number of pieces.

'How do you do? I've been wanting to meet you again.' Clarissa had often felt Stephen might be the catalyst to the whole damned enigma, but rumours of his continued service on the Continent scotched any such considerations. But if Stephen were still in the country then Marianne might not be far away either. Clarissa allowed the options to run swiftly through her mind. Elopement, abduction, even that he'd offered her a *carte blanche*. Each option was rejected as unlikely almost as soon as she conceived it.

'How do you do, ma'am?' Stephen executed another polite little bow and turned towards Caroline.

Clarissa risked another glance at her companion before she made the introduction. Did Caroline know about Stephen? She didn't recall she'd mentioned the name to her, but Richard might have done so. The pair of them must have spoken of the matter when they were alone together.

'Lady Burnett,' she continued, politely introducing the pair automatically while her brain cogitated on how to rid herself of her friend.

'Ma'am.' The lad executed another bow, and with a final, awkward glance at Clarissa's profile, made his apologies in form. 'It is most unfortunate, but I must beg you to allow me to leave. I have a most pressing engagement to attend.' A final flourish and he turned to walk away.

Clarissa's next move startled Caroline as much as the lad himself. Almost without thinking, she stepped smartly to his side and slipped an arm gently under his own. There was no way she was going to let the youthful officer out of her sight while he remained the missing link in her puzzle.

'I'm going your way myself,' she told him, airily waving a dismissal to Leighton's sister who looked as though she was preparing to make an attempt to stop her. 'Perhaps you'll be good enough to escort me.'

'Oh … Ah.'

'Marianne is in the greatest danger,' she hissed quietly in his ear in an attempt to still his faltering protests.

'Of course, ma'am.' He reacted to the name quickly, and though he quizzed her with his eyes, made no attempt to engage her in conversation until they were out of Caroline's earshot.

'Who the devil are you?' He started the interrogation while Leighton's sister stared after them, still undecided what she should do. Leighton would never forgive her if any harm came to Clarissa, and yet, though she'd known the girl for no more than a few weeks, she seemed to have a decided mind of her own. What could she do if Clarissa made up her mind to accompany the gentleman? Walk with her? The girl had clearly warned her off that notion.

'Be quiet.' Clarissa could imagine the thoughts whirling around her friend's brain, but Stephen was the first solid lead she'd found since Sophie had fled. She was determined not to mishandle him and, in her opinion, the lad would admit nothing to any wider audience than Marianne's twin. She steered him adroitly around a corner and into a narrow alleyway, noting that he limped heavily. An old war wound perhaps.

'Please, ma'am, I must insist.'

The pressure on Clarissa's arm persuaded her he was in earnest and she allowed him to bring their progress to a halt.

'I am Marianne's twin sister, Clarissa,' she told him, all too aware that in relating her name she was committing the ultimate sin if he turned out to be anyone other than the man she sought. 'The real question,' she continued, 'is who you are, and what you know of my sister's whereabouts?'

He didn't answer, but caught up her arm again and hurried her through the alley and towards a further wide street despite his limp, which seemed to be bothering him more and more. A swift glance up and down the roadway, and they'd crossed it, slipped down another alley and emerged into a stretch of greenery that was oddly familiar. She glanced around and recognized they were in the same park from which Marianne had disappeared, though at the far end from that she was familiar with. A much more remote and lonely spot too.

'What do you want?' The lad sounded desperate, but Clarissa fought down any qualms she may have felt. He wasn't dangerous. Not to her, at any rate. She was sure of that.

'My sister, Marianne. Do you know where she is?' She saw the emotions openly displayed on his face and the lie that bubbled to the surface.

'No. You have the wrong man.'

'The truth please,' she returned, desperation lending countenance to her refutation. 'You can't know what trouble she's in.'

'I must know,' he temporized. 'How can I tell if you're truly her sister?'

'I'm her twin, look at me,' railed Clarissa. 'We are as alike as two peas in a pod. Tell me. I must know, is she hurt?'

Her desperation seemed to convince the lad and he quietly capitulated. 'I'll take you to her. It's not far.' Once he'd made the decision he opened up and treated Clarissa as the sister she was. 'I couldn't reveal her whereabouts until I was sure,' he admitted. 'She is presently living alone with me and would have lost her reputation if it became known. Also there is another reason.'

'Lord Leighton.'

'You know of him?' The lad's face was grim. 'If news of this escapade comes to his ears then her future will be bleak indeed. He's the most insufferable creature alive, and the very thought of him drives her to distraction.'

Clarissa laughed. The thought of Leighton driving anyone to distraction was absurd, most especially her strong-willed sister.

'It's true, I assure you.' The lad turned a most serious countenance on her. 'You must not think anything out of the ordinary has happened either. I've been too weak until quite recently to make an attempt on her honour even if I were of a mind to do so.'

Stephen looked so earnest that Clarissa was well on the way to forgiving him until she considered her sister's plight.

'You did her reputation no service,' was all she could vouchsafe, 'but Leighton won't hear of it from me. Where is she?'

By this time they'd emerged from the park and were approaching a ramshackle structure set in its own, badly neglected grounds.

Stephen, somewhat stiffly, indicated a mouldering doorway that led on to a staircase. The smell inside was vaguely reminiscent of boiled cabbage and onion, but Clarissa made no attempt to hold back. There was another doorway at the head of the stairs and she stumbled through its dim portals into a room that had evidently been freshly cleaned and tidied. A familiar figure turned from the window and stared at her.

'Clarissa!'

'Marianne.'

The two sisters clung together for several minutes before Marianne roused herself to take charge.

'How's your leg, Stephen? Can you walk a while further?' Her voice held more than sisterly affection and Clarissa's eyes opened wider. The pair were in love, truly the one situation she hadn't expected to face, and one that could prove to be the ruin of them all.

'I'll be back before dark,' he conceded and bowed in his stiff way to Clarissa. 'Talk some sense into her,' he requested.

'Sense?' Clarissa turned to her twin, perplexed.

'He doesn't know what he's saying.' Marianne dismissed the question easily. 'I don't have any refreshment to offer you,' she told her sister, then laughed and embraced her again. 'I'm truly glad to see you, but how are you here in London?'

'Aunt Eleanor took me in,' answered Clarissa. 'She was missing one of the Miss Meredews, and once she'd seen how alike we were, the other would do as well.'

'How like her to be so madly scatterbrain. Have you passed muster amongst my friends?'

'Largely, but you've yet to explain how you come to be living here. I understand Stephen is your only companion.'

'Dreadful, isn't it? To be left alone with a man who could seduce you.' Marianne gaily laughed off the slur. 'The truth of the matter is, that until the last day or two he was too weak to harm my reputation, and is sadly backward in doing so now. He is too much the gentleman, though I fear society will view it differently. Is he not magnificent though?'

'He might be,' conceded Clarissa uncertainly, though she considered his conduct argued no such thing. 'I gather from your words you've acted as his nurse all these weeks?'

'I had to, for who else would?' Marianne's tone might have sounded somewhat melodramatic to one who knew her less well than her sister. 'He was set upon quite close by and left for dead; indeed would have died if we hadn't come upon him. A gang of vicious bullies had attacked him with cudgels, urged on by Lord Dalwinton, the most thoroughly evil man I've ever met.'

'Stephen looked in remarkable health to me.'

'Only let me tell you the whole and you'll understand,' Marianne interrupted her sister. 'Stephen, as I think I wrote you, is the heroic young man who protected me from Lord Dalwinton's advances.'

'I don't see—'

'You will. Following our initial meeting, I continued to see him off and on at parties, and though always surrounded by others we began to fall deeply in love.'

'You were promised to Lord Leighton.' Clarissa gasped at the impropriety of her sister's conduct, then began to blush when she recalled her own perfidious conduct with the man she regarded as her sister's future husband.

'It was never formally announced,' the little girl in Marianne pouted, 'and my feelings replicate those foretold in the most romantic of novels. Oh Clarissa, I knew at once I could never go through with such a shameful engagement, not once I'd felt true love at last. You must know Lord Leighton was the biggest catch on the marriage mart and I accepted him only for his position.

How green and foolish I was then, how little I knew my own heart.'

'What of Leighton's feelings?'

'Stephen was due to leave for France to rejoin his regiment.' Marianne ignored her sister's plea, freely mixing her story with fulsome praise for her young lover. 'He felt quite as he ought, I assure you. Until such a time as I was free from Leighton, he would not, could not, declare himself, but he wished to bid me farewell in more private surroundings than we frequently found ourselves.'

Clarissa thought back on the times Richard had wanted to be private with her. Well, he'd contrived easily enough, even at society parties, and so would Marianne she was sure. However, she could sympathize with such a lover's tryst as Marianne was mapping out. After all, Richard had arranged as much for her at Caroline's house.

'I took Sophie along to the assignation, she's been a darling and we've lacked for nothing all these weeks.'

Clarissa wasn't so sure of that. The girl's plain duty lay in telling her employers where Marianne was, not shielding her from exposure. In not following her duty, she might very well have contributed to ruining the reputation of the very mistress she professed to love. Evidently she hadn't thought to tell Marianne her sister was in London either. Had she done so then the entire charade might have been brought to an early completion.

'Don't look so stern, Clarissa, my dear. I tell you, I had no option, nor Sophie either.' Marianne collected her thoughts and returned to the story.

'We came upon Stephen at the very moment the blackguards attacked him. I didn't see Dalwinton at first, only my own brave love, attempting to parry their vicious assault with no more than his cane. It was a poor weapon and he was vastly outnumbered, but he defended himself courageously. I could see it was a hopeless contest, and in the end I ran forward to stop the affray. Sophie was at my heels, but the damage had already been done. Poor Stephen slumped to the ground while they continued to beat and kick him, only desisting when I threw myself over his body.'

This was one act Clarissa could imagine. She knew her sister to be utterly fearless when it came to defending those she loved. It sounded as though she'd been foolish as well.

'Sophie too, flung herself fearlessly into the fight. I believe they would have thrust me out of the way and continued to beat Stephen if she hadn't run at them whirling my reticule around her head. They ran off then, vicious cowards one and all, and that's when I saw him: Dalwinton – standing a short way off with his damnable valet, both of them laughing at the damage those thugs had done. Aye, and paying them off in full sight of us.'

'I gather Stephen wasn't as dead as you feared.' Clarissa attempted to lead her sister back to the story.

'No, but he was badly beaten and for days afterwards I feared he might die at any moment.'

'Why didn't you bring in a doctor and have him nursed properly? Aunt Eleanor would have called on her own physician for you. Stephen would have been better off if he lay anywhere else than this hovel.'

'Dalwinton!' Marianne accused. 'He spoke to me directly before he left. He cursed his minions who wouldn't stoop to harming a lady and threatened to finish Stephen off himself. Indeed, he might have done so if Sophie hadn't stood up to him. I had no one I could trust other than her, and with Stephen dying in my arms, I could barely think of what to do next.

'Sophie was so staunch and she arranged it all. One of her relatives owns the property and was content to rent out this room and aid us in the task of carrying Stephen in. It's not as comfortable as I'd like, nor as spacious, but under the circumstances I had no option. It was a safe haven for us. A doctor was sent to attend Stephen's wounds, not perhaps a man of the first respectability, but kind to us and unlikely to mention the matter to Dalwinton. For the rest, Sophie saw to it that all our needs were met.'

'What about Stephen? Didn't he have anything to say about your situation?' Clarissa had thought the lad was a gentleman at the least.

'As to that, you may think yourself as one with him. I can see you're horrified to think I'd risk my reputation, as was he. I don't think it, and I never will. While Stephen was still in peril of his life, I couldn't leave him. Nor could he send me away, when he was still comatose.'

'And now? He's recovered his strength, but you remain closeted here. Is he still in peril?'

'He's in the greatest danger, Clarissa. Dalwinton is out for revenge. He's too much the coward to fight man to man, but he'd have been all too pleased to see Stephen die there and then. I'm convinced he'll take advantage of any opportunity to complete the job. As to my love, he continued to flit in and out of consciousness for more than a week, and even later, when he was awake, he lay for days in a fever, raving. I just couldn't bring myself to leave him, not even if Sophie herself should engage to nurse him.'

Clarissa reached out a hand to comfort her sister, who was beginning to sob at the memories stored up. Marianne caught hold of her emotions, however, and continued to speak.

'By the time he'd regained his health well enough to understand what was happening, it was too late to mend my reputation. He knew as well as I that I was hopelessly compromised. Not that it mattered in the least because he intended to marry me anyway, despite his lack of prospects. He was elevated first to lieutenant, then to a captaincy, gazetted in the field for outstanding bravery under fire, but with the wars in France at an end, his promotions may not be confirmed by the Department for War. He would then revert to the rank of ensign, for he has no money of his own to purchase a commission.'

Clarissa found a new respect for the abilities of the young officer. For two such heady promotions to have been earned on the battlefield he must not only have been fearless, but an extremely talented leader of men.

'I should have returned to Aunt Eleanor's protection long since, despite the damage to my reputation, and so Stephen is forever telling me. When I was nursing a helpless invalid there can have been no impropriety, but I cannot leave him even now, when I'm terrified Dalwinton will make another attempt on his life. Leighton also; if he learns we've been closeted together for so long, he may well call Stephen out. He's a crack shot and accounted a swordsman of some merit.' Marianne sobbed out loud in her fear. 'Stephen is as brave as a lion, and would never back down from such a challenge.'

'I don't believe Leighton will challenge Stephen to a duel.' Clarissa smiled, holding back her real reasons for thinking so. 'Only think of how foolish that would make him appear. For either you or he to cry off is one thing, and it has to be admitted it could cause a stir in some quarters, but a duel is quite another. That would argue a far more serious rift, and while the gossip in its wake may ruin you, it would also make him a laughing stock.'

'I cannot go back to Aunt Eleanor now, Clarissa. While I was nursing a helpless invalid, there could have been some scope for forgiveness, but I've been away far too long. The gossip must already have started.'

'I've taken your place, remember? I was accepted by society at large, and by all your friends too. Even Leighton. There is no gossip, nor need there ever be.'

'Your sister's quite right, Marianne.' Stephen had returned and was standing in the shadows and had been listening to their conversation for longer than either of them knew. 'You must make your return to society. If Leighton will release you from your vows then we'll be wed as soon as we may. I went to the War Office today and reported back for duty. They were sympathetic to my injuries, but I must leave for the Continent within the week.'

'Stephen, you—' Marianne's attempt to debate the issue was brought to an abrupt stand when the young officer ignored her arguments and turned instead to her sister, Clarissa.

'Can you arrange for Marianne to return to her family with no scandal attached?' he asked.

'I believe so.'

'Then it's best done quick. I've been at my wit's end trying to think of a way out of this unholy imbroglio. We plan to marry as soon as we can, but it wouldn't do for her situation here to become known. My mother died when I was young and my father, a man of the cloth, succumbed to the influenza not long after I joined up, so I have no family to escort her to, and neither can I leave her in this house until the deed is done. The neighbourhood is not respectable, nor one in which a lady should reside alone. You, too, must leave us in good time; the evening is closing in and it's already beginning to grow dark. I fear the streets here, disagreeable as they are during the day, only grow rougher with the onset of night.'

'I'll arrange matters for you,' promised Clarissa. 'There are others I must consult, those who already know of the deception being practised. A day at most. I'll return here tomorrow, but, as you say, I must leave for home immediately before my own absence is commented upon.'

Clarissa's farewells to her sister were short lived, but inevitably attended by some tears, shed in equal measure by each of the twins. Stephen saw her out and escorted her on her way.

'You should have insisted Marianne leave you as soon as you recovered your senses,' she accused him once they had left the house.

'I know,' he replied. His eyes were unable to return her gaze and he dropped his head. 'I did speak to her, I promise you I did, but she wouldn't attend to me.' He flushed. 'I don't mean to excuse myself,' he told her in a small voice, 'or my scandalous behaviour in allowing her to stay with me under such circumstances. The truth, if it must be told, was that having her so close was as sweet to me as staying was to her.'

'I doubt if she'd let you send her away,' Clarissa agreed with him reluctantly. What would she herself do if it was Leighton in trouble? 'She always was the more wilful of us twins.'

'This is the way.' Stephen motioned towards the narrow opening that led into the park, but Clarissa begged him to return forthwith to Marianne.

'It's getting darker by the minute and I can find my way from here,' she told him readily. 'Walking the streets alone at night might be unusual conduct in a lady, but to be caught in the company of a strange gentleman in such a place would outrage all propriety.' And she strode off into the dark with an airy wave, determined to bespeak a hackney as soon as she reached the more respectable streets on the far side of the park.

*

Clarissa was halfway across the greensward, in plain sight of the streets she knew so well, when she realized she was being followed. She turned to face her pursuer, more or less certain it was Stephen following in her wake despite her denials, and only realized her mistake when a black shadow sprang on her out of the gloom.

Afterwards she could only recall the brief vision of an arm raised high before something exploding on her skull. Then she was falling, a black tunnel closing in on her vision.

CHAPTER SEVENTEEN

Clarissa Imprisoned

larissa didn't remain unconscious for long. She was
vaguely aware of someone lifting her; a big man, and strong
enough to throw her over his shoulder without exerting a significant effort. She stilled herself, some sentient sixth sense warning
her not to betray her wakefulness. She would stand more chance
of evading her captors if she retained the advantage of surprise.

The others walked behind, sufficiently far to the rear she
couldn't quite catch what they were saying. Two only, she
decided, but couldn't be sure; one whose voice was familiar,
and far more refined than any footpad had the right to own. She
nearly betrayed herself when she recognized the tones, for Lord
Dalwinton was amongst her captors! She told herself she
shouldn't have been surprised; she'd known the man was
searching through the neighbourhood, knew he suspected her
part in the deception. Knew too, he was looking for the proof.
What the devil did he want with her?

How can I escape? Should I scream? Not until I see someone,
she decided, thinking through a fog. Her head hurt abominably, and she would have slipped back into unconsciousness
if she hadn't been laid so uncomfortably over the man's

shoulder. Suddenly she was tumbling like a sack of coal and shrieking out while she thrust out her arms to break her fall. She hit a wooden surface with a resounding crash and immediately struggled up into a seated position, thankful she'd fallen no more than a few feet.

'Get your head down, miss.' The giant seemed friendly enough, for all he was aiding her enemies. Then, when she didn't react, he cuffed her gently as a reminder who was boss and she fell back.

Her shocked brain told her she shouldn't obey his orders so docilely, for all there seemed no option, but she couldn't think of anything else to do. In fact she was still no more than half-conscious and couldn't have remained sitting upright for much longer even if she'd a mind to.

A greasy, muck-strewn tarpaulin was flung over her prone body and the cart she'd been tipped into began to move in sickening lurches down the pot-holed roadway. Not far, perhaps a half-mile at most. Too much for Clarissa though, for she fell back into her stupor.

The giant unloaded her without ceremony, but displayed a rough hewn gentleness that suggested he wasn't entirely in sympathy with her kidnapping. His words seemed to back up those sentiments.

'We ought not to deal with abducting the gentry, Jem. Likely as not her friends'll be out searching soon. Won't do for them to find her here.' He set her down gently and held on to her until she found her feet. 'You'll do, miss,' he assured her. 'Not far to walk now.'

Another man interrupted him, a more educated voice with bitter overtones. 'You hold your tongue, young Ned. Lord Dalwinton's paying us well to house this chit safe and sound. Safe from us at any rate.'

'You're a fool, Jem. Dalwinton's not the man to back you up if the Runners come calling.'

'Hush, man. I told you to hold your tongue. He's not a cove to cross either. You'll be dead meat in spite of your size if he hears you speak against him.'

Clarissa, her head still swirling, leaned against the cart and attempted to look around, barely acknowledging the argument. It was too dark to mark any detail, but they were in a closed yard which smelt of stale beer and horse manure, both of which were conspiring to make her feel violently ill. The smaller of the two men, though she could barely see their features in the gloom, seemed to be staring at her. He spoke again at last.

'Safe for now, at least. She won't be so proud once Lord Dalwinton's through with her.' He sighed gustily. 'Leave her be Ned, she can walk by herself.' The giant had stooped as though to carry her again, but obediently straightened up once his elder had spoken.

'Come along, miss. Not far now,' he told her gently.

'Don't try to fool us either, lady. There's no way out of here for you.' The man called Jem was evidently the superior in their partnership and intended to have his authority acknowledged.

The way forward led through a thick oak door, which was locked and bolted behind them, and up a narrow, winding staircase. The scent of stale beer and tobacco intensified and she gained the notion she was in a common ale house, probably situated in the stews. They climbed higher and a curiously sweet smell began to overlay the heavier scents of the ale. Another door barred their way and she was unceremoniously thrust through it.

The sole lighting in Clarissa's new surroundings came from a single, stinking tallow candle, which guttered and flickered alarmingly. The door slammed shut behind her and she stumbled forward, suddenly aware of a face, Lord Dalwinton's, barely lit by the candle's feeble light. Another figure closed in behind her to guard the doorway and she felt a moment of despair.

'I wonder which Marianne we've captured?' Dalwinton purred out the words in a velvet undertone, but he seemed to be talking to himself for no answer was forthcoming from his silent companion. He, Clarissa suspected, had to be the rogue's valet.

'Or is there only one of you, after all?' Lord Dalwinton continued, laughing unpleasantly. Then, in a sudden change of mood, he stepped forward to take Clarissa's chin firmly in his hand, and held up her head as though to study her face more thoroughly.

Since she and Marianne were so exactly alike in their features, Clarissa seriously doubted whether even someone who knew them intimately could have told them apart just by looking. In the Stygian gloom of a barely lit attic the base nobleman stood no chance of doing so. She spat in his face.

The resultant slap knocked her clean off her feet, but, some-what oddly, seemed to clear her head rather than amplify her dizziness. She rose immediately and faced her tormentor with a bravado she was far from feeling.

'You won't be so satisfied with yourself when Leighton discovers you've abducted me,' she told him with a sudden rush of confidence.

'I'm already at issue with your lover, my dear,' Dalwinton acknowledged. 'He, too, will discover what it means to cross me before long.' He stared at her for several seconds before he continued his monologue. 'You are very alike. Are you truly Marianne? Or just a common deceiver?' His voice was soft, but there was a hint of menace apparent in it that chilled the girl to her bones.

Clarissa made no answer, but stood tall and raised her head proudly, her eyes flashing defiance.

'It matters but little, either way,' Dalwinton drawled easily. 'Perhaps you're just a silly young chit who's made a fool of him by taking up with a soldier boy, or maybe he's foisted his own deception upon society. Whichever it is, he'll be made to play the cuckold in front of the ton.' He laughed again and tapped her lightly on the cheek, chuckling wickedly when she recoiled. 'You'll talk to me, my dear, believe me, you will. I'll enjoy the interrogation too, but not just yet. Most unfortunately for my plans, I have an engagement I must keep.' He raised his head and rapped out a command. 'Marston.'

'Yes, sir.'

'Bind her and make certain the door is locked.' Dalwinton was already striding towards the exit when he turned to further instruct his underling, 'I'll have your hide if she escapes.'

'No chance of that, sir.' Marston advanced on Clarissa with a twisted skein of rope in his hands.

'Don't you dare lay your hands on me.' Dalwinton had gone and Clarissa stood straight, bravely meeting the servant's stare. Perhaps she could overawe the man by acting the *grande dame*.

'You heard the master,' Marston laughed at her play-acting. 'You ain't the first woman he's had up here, nor likely to be the last. Don't matter what airs you play off on me, my lady, you're going to be secured, and you have my word on it. Hold out your hands like a good little girl or I'll come and get them myself and you won't like that.'

Numbly Clarissa did as she was bid, crossing her wrists in front of her body. Marston was quite capable of forcing her, and the deed would be done in a far more undignified manner.

'No!' she shrieked out loud when he tipped her on to the

floor and swept her skirts off her ankles. A deft loop and he was tying them together too.

'I'm leaving you now, miss,' he told her, 'but I'll remain on guard downstairs with Ned. Ain't no other way out of this room, that's why the gov'nor uses it.'

'What about something to eat? I'm starving.'

'I doubt that,' he returned, 'but I'll get one of the girls to bring something up later.'

'What about the candle?' She watched the dim flame eating away at the tallow and shuddered. It wouldn't last much longer.

'You can have that,' he conceded, and left her to her own devices.

It didn't take Clarissa long to discover that Marston's knots were tied fast. She'd tried to separate her wrists while he bound her, but he'd had too much experience to be fooled by such a raw girl's trick, and he had drawn the rope tight before he knotted it.

She searched around her prison, taking in as much as she could from her prone position, hoping to find a sharp edge on which to sever the bonds. As she soon realized, there was so such thing. Perhaps she could burn through the rope with the candle. She eyed it hopefully, twisting and turning her hands to discover whether she could find any point loose enough for the flame to sear the rope and not her tender skin. There wasn't and, deprived of any hope of freeing herself in that manner, she drew herself up into a seated position, supported by the wall.

The room she occupied was longer than it was wide and tapered towards the only doorway through which her gaoler had vanished. It was boarded all around, not even a window to break the monotony, and although the wood smelt strongly of rot and damp, it was evidently still in reasonable repair. The floor was wooden too, its ancient timbers heaving over the rafters beneath like the swell of a sea frozen in time. The roof was solid, and far too high for her to access when there was no furniture in the room. She settled back and began to plan her escape.

In actual fact, none of her plans amounted to anything. The devil was in the detail, for all of them depended on her hands and feet being free, and none of them could get her past the guard on the stairway – nor even past her first obstacle, the locked door to her cell.

The candle guttered and went out, leaving her in absolute darkness. No, not absolute, as she quickly realized. The floor-boards had shrunk over the centuries since the ale house had been built and chinks of pale light were visible here and there. She shuffled across to the far corner where the boards were particularly unsound and laid her eye to a narrow crack. The room beneath was dimly lit and appeared to be occupied with rough beds or bunks, one or two of which were in use, though their occupants lay still as though unconscious. The heavy, sweet, sickly scent of incense cloyed in her nostrils, over-whelming the stench of rotten wood and the all-pervading damp. Opium: the thought ran into her head from nowhere. She was held fast in an opium den.

The rattle of a key in the door brought her back to her senses and she swiftly shuffled away from her spy-hole when a servant girl appeared with a trencher of bread and cheese, and a heavy pewter mug filled to the brim with some sort of foaming ale. Marston stood immediately behind her, holding up a branch of candles, and Clarissa immediately held up her hands for his inspection. The appeal was by no means less effective for being mute. Clearly the manservant's prisoner would be unable to eat unless he removed her bonds.

'Stay with her while she eats,' he warned the serving wench, and set about freeing Clarissa's bonds. Then he lay down the candles and retreated towards the stairs with a final admonition, 'See you tie her securely again and lock the door. I'll be up to check on her once I've seen to my own meal.' Then to his prisoner, 'I may be gone, but Ben's still on watch, and Jem too. There's no escape for the likes of you, even if you succeed in overpowering the girl.'

Since Clarissa had immediately taken stock of the servant-girl's broad figure and decided she'd come off the worst in any violent encounter, she'd already discounted this method of escape. Thus his words had little effect on her. She fell on the bread and cheese as though she really were starving, and even sipped a mouthful or two of the filthy looking brew, which tasted as foul as it looked.

'Where are we?' she asked, anxious to obtain any information that might aid her escape.

'Don't matter much to you, my love.' The girl's voice was slurred by the drink that reeked on her breath, but she didn't seem particularly unsympathetic to Clarissa's plight. 'Once Lord Dalwinton's got you in his power you're lost, as many a wench has found. Jem won't help you either, for all he owns the place lock, stock and barrel.'

'You don't like Dalwinton?' That much was obvious, as was the fact that the servant girl feared him.

'If he wants something from you, my love, you see you give it to him quick. He's a nasty streak in him, that one, and he'll enjoy forcing it out of you. Once you've served his purpose, you'll be left no better than me. Drink and drugs, enough to get you snared, then you won't be too high and mighty to do his bidding, even if it's to please a man.'

Clarissa had already worked that one out for herself.

Dalwinton was in too deep to ever allow her to return to society; abduction, with the probable threat of torture to follow! He'd be ruined if even a tithe of her story was believed. Her too, of course, and Marianne with her.

She'd finished, and subserviently held out her hands to be bound again, gambling that the servant girl wouldn't be as adept at binding her as Marston. Clarissa swiftly decided she was right to make that assumption when the girl began to twine the rope around her wrists. Far too loose to be effective, she'd be able to free herself in no time.

'Please,' she begged piteously. 'Leave me one candle to light the room. I'm frightened of the rats.'

'Here you are then, my love.' The girl set one of the candles on the floor, steadying it in the sticky mess of tallow left by the dead one Marston had allowed her. 'Won't do you much good, mind. It'll be out in an hour.'

Clarissa didn't care. Marston would be back to check on her bonds long before that happened. She had less than an hour available to gain her freedom, quite possibly much less.

'The drink too,' she requested. 'I can lie down and lap at it if I get thirsty.'

The girl nodded and duly did as she was bid, before walking out and locking the door behind her.

As soon as she was left alone, Clarissa began to work on her bonds, twisting her wrists and biting into the knotted rope with the renewed strength of desperation. Just as she'd speculated, the girl had left her no more than loosely tied, and within a few minutes she was shaking the last of the knots off her wrists. With her hands loose, her nimble fingers went to work on the ropes that held her ankles, and it wasn't long before she was completely free of her bonds.

She listened at the door, but though she could hear nothing, she didn't seek to advertise her freedom by checking the latch when she'd clearly heard the key turn. Instead she slipped quietly across the room and began to work on the loose floor-boards in the corner, employing her fingertips in lieu of a suitable tool. A rotten piece tore away in her hands and she used it as a lever, throwing her weight on to the fragile wood until it splintered beneath her.

No matter, the floorboard had loosened further, the crack was now a small hole, but big enough for her purposes. Clarissa fed the lighted candle through the aperture and let it drop, delighted when it struck one of the cots directly below, over-turning on to the blanket that covered it. A faint skein of evil-smelling smoke began to arise from the thick, greasy mate-rial, which commenced to blacken around the candle, and eventually burst into flame.

Clarissa continued to pray the blaze wouldn't be noticed while the minutes passed, and the flame burned more fiercely, sending her spirits crashing into the depths when it guttered, then of a sudden, elation, when it grew into a fire and finally, with its momentum assured, into a conflagration.

The girl retrieved her drink, and measured the heavy mug in her hands. Satisfied by its weight, she flung the contents across the floor and began to slam it against the door, screaming out with all the youthful power of her lungs.

'Fire!' she shouted. 'Fire!'

The far corner of the room was beginning to let in a haze of smoke through the splintered floorboard and, as time passed by, more faint tendrils began to appear through other weak spots. A hint of scarlet showed in the thicker smoke and Clarissa began to panic. Had she miscalculated? Surely someone must have noticed the fire by now, but would they bother to save her?

'Fire!' She renewed her hammering on the thick oak door and

listened carefully, screwing her courage up for the task ahead. She could hear heavy boots echoing on the wooden treads.

The key turned in the door, the latch sprung and the door opened.

Clarissa swung the heavy mug with all her might and Marston staggered crazily across the floor, dropping heavily on all fours while he shook his head to rid it of the haze of swirling darkness that threatened to overcome him.

He was bleeding freely from a cut on his forehead, but Clarissa had no time to note that before she was on the stairs and racing down with scant respect for their uneven treads. At the halfway point, blinded by the smoke which added to the night to render the stairway barely visible, she collided heavily with someone ascending. She had no way of knowing, but that person was the owner, Jem. They both staggered and fell, rolling and slipping down the stairs in a heap of flailing limbs. The door at the bottom was open and Clarissa, the first to recover, flung herself through it with a cry of triumph.

'Not likely, young miss.' The giant who'd first imprisoned her caught her in a fast embrace.

The end, though unexpected, was swift, catching Clarissa by surprise as much as her captor.

A second figure appeared, tall and broad of shoulder, with something familiar in his silhouette. He was evidently intending to come to her rescue and the young giant realized this at the very same moment she did. He thrust his captive to one side and turned to meet his new adversary.

The newcomer held the advantage of surprise, however, and delivered a powerful punch before his opponent had time to cover up. Clarissa wasn't entirely *au fait* with the sport of boxing, but even she could see how effective the hit was. Her huge captor was as strong as an ox, as she had good reason to know, but he staggered under the blow and fell back before his antagonist.

'Clarissa.' The newcomer motioned her to stand aside when his game adversary came back at him and attempted a round-house swing that would have taken his head off had it connected.

The giant, unbalanced by his opponent's adroit evasion, immediately suffered from the immediate and skilful response to his lapse. A scything hook to his short ribs brought him up short; a perfectly executed right cross that looked like to fell him, left him staggering, with his brain in a tither; and a cross buttock throw finally saw him sent to the ground.

'Richard.' Clarissa flung herself into her saviour's arms and began to sob with relief.

CHAPTER EIGHTEEN

Explanations Due

The building was well alight by this time, and although it didn't look as though anyone would be troubling them, Leighton acted quickly to spirit Clarissa away from the inferno.

He had a closed carriage waiting at the entrance to the yard, with Tom holding his place at the horses' heads, and, while her lover assisted Clarissa into the vehicle, two other men closed in behind them. She immediately recognized Richard's preferred tiger, Teddy, and one of Caroline's footmen, the very lad who'd accompanied them on the abortive shopping trip earlier that day. Both were armed with vicious looking horse pistols and stout cudgels, and looked as though they were prepared to use them. No wonder no one was prepared to take up the chase.

'Perhaps you can tell me what's been going on.' Richard had climbed into the vehicle with her and began the questioning as soon as they started to move. 'I've been in the devil of a pucker since I discovered you were missing. This is a dangerous part of the city for green girls to explore.'

'I was abducted.' Clarissa found herself curiously calm. She had a story to tell, but it couldn't involve her sister until she'd ensured Marianne's reputation would be left untarnished. 'Lord

Dalwinton and his thugs took me unawares and imprisoned me in the attics of that filthy ale house, and I'm not the first to be incarcerated there, or so I'm informed.' She stared directly at Leighton. 'Did you know it was an opium den, too?' She frowned. 'In fact, how did you know I was there at all? Surely Dalwinton himself didn't admit to kidnapping me.'

'No. I haven't seen him. Yet.' Richard's face was dark with anger at the dastardly antics of his fellow nobleman and he was determined to put an end to his schemes, by whatever means proved necessary. Even so, he was aware that Clarissa was missing out some vital parts of the tale.

'We have John, Caroline's young footman, to thank for your safe return,' he carried on, outwardly calm. 'When you went off with your young friend.' He stopped and regarded her quizzically. 'Who was he, by the way?'

'Stephen.' Clarissa knew she was giving away too much with the name, but she had to give him an answer of some sort. Although she was determined to hold back certain information, she wasn't prepared to lie to Leighton, even for the sake of her beloved sister. He didn't deserve that.

'Marianne's new swain, I apprehend. Are they living together?' He stared at Clarissa's face, meeting her mock innocent gaze with a testing examination of his own. 'No matter,' he decided at length. 'Caroline saw you couldn't be stopped, but neither did she intend to leave you alone with a lad she didn't recognize. She retrieved the parcels from John and sent him after you. I gather from him that you were led to a somewhat dilapidated house in the suburbs, from which you emerged several hours later, and it was while you attempted to cross the park alone you were attacked.'

'No fault of Stephen's,' admitted Clarissa, thankful her sister's part in the affair wasn't going to be challenged. 'He escorted me as far as the park and would have remained at my side all the way home if I'd allowed it. It was I who thought it best to return alone. A single woman escorted by a man that late in the evening would hardly have been thought seemly if anyone had spotted us.' She smiled ingenuously. 'It seemed very likely that someone would see us together in the more respectable districts.'

'Ah, I see. You may accompany a man you've never before met to a remote house without even a maid to keep you company, and yet your propriety is offended when he offers to escort you home.' Leighton let his shattered feelings show. 'You must forgive me for thinking that the both of you are to blame.'

'Hardly. Stephen is still weak from his wounds, and he could never have fought off the dastardly footpads who abducted me even if he'd been fully recovered. Dalwinton would have seen to that.'

'He was wounded?' Leighton's eyebrows rose again in surprise. 'Indeed, now I come to think of it, Caroline described him as lame in one leg. An old war wound, I suppose?'

'Another story entirely,' Clarissa returned evasively. 'I gather your sister's footman continued to follow in my tracks once I'd been taken.'

'He was too far back to interfere in your assault, largely due to avoiding Stephen on his return, but he freely admitted there were too many for any intervention to have been successful. He shadowed your journey as best he could, but lost you again when you were transported into the yard in which I found you. He waited around outside for an hour or two, then decided you must have been locked up for the night and returned to tell Caroline where you were. Fortunately I was with her, and the rest you know.'

Clarissa could imagine the rescue party steaming to her aid, and took up the story from her own point of view, describing both her incarceration and eventual escape, much to his amusement when he learned of how she'd deliberately set the building alight.

'There's something you're not telling me,' he questioned her gently. They were nearing the Markhams' house and he feared he might never know the whole if he didn't do something quickly. Clarissa was absurdly fond of her twin sister, and was entirely capable of swapping places at a moment's notice. Once Marianne had returned to live with the Markhams the whole imbroglio would spawn more complex issues.

'I cannot betray my sister,' returned Clarissa brokenly.

'Then it was Marianne,' he decided, without any real surprise in his voice, and promptly began to kiss her.

'Richard, no.' Clarissa was allowed no more than a moment to catch her breath before he took her tenderly in his arms once more and commenced to kissing her thoroughly again. Though not averse to his masterly charms, she couldn't help feeling his love-making was designed to make her tell the whole. As she most certainly should, she couldn't help admitting to herself.

'You're right,' she conceded the next time they surfaced, holding up her hands to stop him kissing her again. They were proceeding up the avenue in which the Markhams' house was situated and if she didn't confess it now, God alone knew when she'd have the chance to see him alone again. 'Stephen was beaten near to death by footpads acting for Lord Dalwinton when Marianne came across him. She saved his life and stayed on to nurse him.' The words tumbled out of their own accord, but constituted the major facts.

'An assignation?'

'Yes,' Clarissa nodded. 'Though not an elopement as many may think. The lad was set to return to his regiment and merely wanted to say his goodbyes.'

'He could do that in public,' objected Leighton.

'He ...' Clarissa faltered uneasily, she didn't see why she should excuse his conduct when she, too, thought it was wrong-headed of him to have done so, and all the more despicable was Marianne's behaviour in assenting to the scheme. Instead, she continued to narrate the story, retelling her sister's story as best she could in the circumstances. 'I suppose you hate her for rejecting you,' she finished. 'I'm sure I can't blame you.'

Leighton laughed. 'I presume I might have in other circum-stances,' he confessed frankly, 'but how could I cavil when her actions brought you into my life? You're the only one I'll ever love, Clarissa, and you're the one I'll marry. There's no reason on earth why we can't be betrothed immediately; she may have her soldier, and you'll be my bride in her stead.'

'We cannot. Oh, please believe me, we cannot.'

'Why ever not?' Leighton dismissed Teddy who was attempting to open the carriage door with an airy wave of his hand. 'Marianne doesn't want me, but I can't believe you don't. You're too unpractised to return my kisses with such passion, and not mean it.'

'I love you,' she told him simply. 'I have done ever since the moment I first met you.'

'Then why?'

'Marianne can never reject your suit, Richard. Not with any propriety. Too many people in society know of your engage-ment, for all it's not been formally announced. If she should do so, then society would compare her to our mother, a married woman running off with her sister-in-law's bridegroom. Like mother, like daughter, and I'd be tainted too. The disgrace would affect us all and Lord Dalwinton would be in a heaven of our own making. You'd be a laughing stock and our repu-tations in tatters.' A single tear ploughed a furrow down her face and she brushed it away angrily. 'Please, we must go in immediately. Uncle John and Aunt Eleanor will be distraught for my safety.'

Leighton nodded and opening the door, handed her down.

'John,' he called out to his sister's footman. 'Please return to Lady Burnett to assure her Miss Meredew is safe and well.'

The Markhams were indeed distraught. They'd just suffered the double blow of having their second niece go missing, neither of them for any good reason they could think of, and were inclined to kill the fatted calf on her return.

The story had to be told again and this time Clarissa missed out no detail of Marianne's miraculous discovery.

The Markhams, though pleased to hear Marianne was safe, were as worried as Clarissa at how Leighton would take the news. Then they were surprised and relieved in equal measure when they found out he'd already discovered Clarissa's deception and forgiven her.

'It's Clarissa, I'll wed,' he told them firmly, to Clarissa's dismay and secret delight, 'and no other. You'd better get used to that idea.'

CHAPTER NINETEEN

A Solution is Expounded

To Clarissa's surprise Lord Leighton called on her early the next morning. She'd been exhausted the previous evening and hadn't yet had the opportunity to discuss Marianne's return to the fold with her aunt and uncle. It must be done today, she told herself, and then, more regretfully, considered her own position. I'll be back home with Aunt Constance by nightfall, she decided.

'My Lord.' Clarissa's greeting was too formal for Leighton's taste when she greeted him in the morning-room.

'My darling would have been more appropriate,' he complained, striding across the room to take her in his arms.

'Richard! The servants will see us,' she protested, but lifted her lips to his kiss anyway.

'They all know we're to be betrothed in a couple of days and no doubt think it most romantic,' he returned carelessly, slipping an arm around her waist and guiding her towards the window. 'Why else do you suppose Downing so forgot his training as to inform you alone of my visit?'

In actual fact the butler had pocketed a handful of fat gold coins not to advise either of the Markhams of the viscount's arrival. He would, in all probability, have allowed the lovers their privacy in any case, but Leighton was a man who liked to make sure of his ground, especially when he was engaged in such clandestine damage limitation.

'How are you feeling this morning?' he continued, holding her face up to the light. 'If it were any other woman of my acquaintance, they'd still be in their beds swallowing a posset or some such thing.' He'd wasted no time in speculating about any such poor spirited action from Clarissa, recognizing immediately that she'd be up with the lark, and raring to begin the ticklish process of sorting out her sister's affairs.

'My head ached abominably last night,' she told him mournfully, 'but I feel fresh as a daisy this morning. There's still some slight swelling where I was hit from behind, but no lingering pain, and I also have a bruise developing under my hair, a souvenir of Lord Dalwinton's assault.' She winced perceptibly when she touched the side of her head where Dalwinton had struck her.

'I intend to pay that cursed blackguard back for that.' Richard looked so menacing and serious that Clarissa added a more humorous rider.

'But worst of all,' she complained, 'is that my nails are ragged and broken from fighting my bonds and those damnable floorboards.'

'You're luckier than you know, Clarissa. You should never have put yourself in such a position.' Leighton was still dwelling seriously on the previous night's events. 'Dalwinton's a fool to resort to kidnapping a woman in your position, but he's still a very dangerous man for all that.'

'I fought fire with fire,' she told him, attempting to charm him out of such an earnest vein.

'You certainly bamboozled him,' Leighton admitted, 'but at what cost if you'd perished in the blaze?'

'Don't remind me; I was in a fair way to believing they'd all flee the conflagration and leave me to die until Marston arrived.'

The viscount laughed suddenly, his eyes sparkling with a different light when he remembered how she'd freed herself. 'Forget my mealy-mouthed words,' he told her. 'You were magnificent.'

'Your tiger is walking your horses.' Clarissa changed the subject abruptly when she turned her head to look through the wide windows that overlooked the square in front of the house. 'I thought you'd rack them up as you usually do. Are you leaving so quickly?'

'We, my darling girl,' he told her with a quizzical look, 'have an assignation this morning. You cannot have forgotten I engaged to show you all the sights? We go out together every morning, and cannot afford to give the gossips an opportunity for idle speculation by abruptly ceasing our excursions without any good reason being made apparent.'

'I have too much to do to waste time driving out with you,' Clarissa objected. 'I still haven't organized the details of Marianne's return, let alone my own dispositions.'

'Then we'll organize together,' he assured her. 'I've already let Downing know we'll be out, and if he should learn you've turned me down, it'll be servant's gossip by tonight.'

'Don't be so foolish.' Clarissa's face broke into a smile for all his bold words. Butler's didn't sink to tittle-tattling with the lower servants, and neither did she believe for a moment that Leighton would have furnished Downing with his plans. 'Where are we supposed to be going?'

'St Paul's.' Leighton drew an arrow at random. An excursion to St Paul's was as good a cover for his real intentions as any.

'We went there two days since,' she told him frankly. They

hadn't, but a venture into the City to take in the wonders of the cathedral had formed that day's cover for their all too real search for her sister, Marianne. 'There must be a hundred other places to take our fancy.'

'As I remember it, you enjoyed your visit to the dome so much, you wished to take another look,' he quizzed her, telling the tale with such a grave face she was forced to laugh out loud.

'Fool,' she accused him.

'Perhaps I am,' Leighton agreed patiently, 'but not such a fool as to allow the Markhams to welcome Marianne back into their home and dispose of you where they will.' He raised his eyebrows questioningly. 'Your Aunt Constance springs instantly to mind?'

'Abominable man. Of course I have to leave. Two Mariannes in the Markhams' household would be one too many for society to bear. Even an identical twin sister would be difficult to explain away, especially if Dalwinton decided to spread his wicked gossip.'

'Lord Dalwinton will be unable to do any such thing,' Richard assured her confidently, 'and neither will you return to Bedfordshire while I draw breath. Are you ready to leave?' He surveyed her attire with a critical, and entirely knowing eye. 'I see you're not,' he decided, 'but let me tell you my horses are too precious to wait around for much longer.'

'Where are we really going?'

'To lend countenance to your sister's liaison with Stephen,' he informed her and, taking hold of her shoulders, spun her around and propelled her towards the door with a playful swat on her behind.

Clarissa squealed out loud and turned reproachful eyes on him, but wisely refrained from the stinging admonition she'd prepared. Instead, she held her head high and swept out of the room, blushing when she realized she'd actually enjoyed the sensation.

Clarissa's toilette was completed in record time, and she returned to the morning-room dressed in charming, if somewhat severe, attire. A dark travelling suit, made up in the military style, complete with epaulettes, matched to stout, leather half boots and a Russian bonnet to hide the bruises that had resulted from her brush with the previous night's thugs.

'Does Teddy know the way?' They were travelling in a closed carriage with his groom driving, rather than the curricle they normally employed, when he usually took the reins himself.

'He does. John's description of the route was most precise.' Richard continued to bring her up to date on his plans. 'We'll take a walk across the park, if you don't mind. I'd rather not advertise our visit to such a run-down house.' He smiled and reassured her. 'There's precious little chance of Dalwinton's men attacking us in broad daylight. Besides, they're more likely to be raking through the ruins of their ale house.'

'Ruins?'

'When I reconnoitred the site earlier this morning the entire building was gutted and smoke still hanging over it, though I couldn't discover that anyone had died as a result of the inferno.'

'I haven't thanked you enough for coming to my rescue,' Clarissa admitted. 'Nor do I see how I ever could.'

'I think something could be arranged,' returned Leighton, and the girl coloured becomingly when she saw the glint in his eyes.

'For all I'd succeeded in escaping the building, I was still in their clutches, and you were very courageous to tackle the man who held me. He's a veritable ox.' Clarissa steered the conversation towards Richard's intervention in order to save her blushes.

'Lucky to catch him unawares you mean,' chuckled Leighton. 'I've watched Ben Fisher at work in the ring. He's only a novice, but if he keeps his nose clean, he's a real prospect for the future. I'd never have caught him out if he'd been in training. Drink and the devil have done for more young fighters than ever their opponents did.'

'But you displayed all the skill of a professional yourself. I'm sure I never expected you to fell him so completely, though Caroline told me you boxed at Cribb's Parlour. I'm not sure what or where that is,' she admitted, 'but I dare say it's a very low place where no female of any sensitivity would ever be seen. Why do you go?'

'So I can tackle men like Ben Fisher, of course,' he replied, with a deprecating laugh. 'Come, we're here. Let me help you down.'

'You're not going to demand satisfaction from Stephen, are you?' Clarissa couldn't help notice that Leighton's countenance had set itself into a more serious vein again.

'A duel. God, no. I can't think why you, or anyone else for that matter, should believe my consequence would be improved by forcing a quarrel on a young greenhorn, and the son of a cleric, moreover.'

The walk through the park was short, and since it wasn't spoiled by any sign of Dalwinton's men, in a very short while they were beating noisily on the filthy and unassuming entrance to Stephen and Marianne's apartment. Stephen himself admitted them with some trepidation, for he was inclined to be over-set by the arrival of his rival on the doorstep, and took good care to shield Marianne from her erstwhile swain.

'I should understand it if you wish to seek satisfaction of me, sir,' he began, all stiff and formal.

'Be a surprise to me if I did,' Leighton dismissed him with a nod and caught Marianne's hand to bring it to his lips in a polite salute. 'By the way,' he began to address Stephen again immediately to save Marianne's blushes, for she was every bit as nervous at meeting Leighton as her suitor. 'I spoke to some people I know at Horse Guards, and they have your promotions in hand.'

'My promotions?'

'I felicitate you, sir. You'll return to your regiment a full blown captain.'

'Thank you, sir,' Stephen stammered, unable to take in his good fortune, or the previously odious Lord Leighton's affability.

'No need to thank me. They had the reports on your actions in front of them. They painted a picture of a damned fine soldier. I did no more than assure them of my patronage.'

'It's more than I deserve.' Stephen looked at the man he'd thought to hate and had the grace to admit his mistake. 'You must think ... Marianne ... Well, sir, none of this whole damned mess is of her making.'

'I doubt that,' returned Leighton cryptically. 'Nor do I doubt you deserve your captaincy or I shouldn't have exerted myself in your favour. For all it would look damned bad if my brother-in-law were to remain a mere ensign when I'd been lionizing his exploits so high.' He clapped the lad on the back. 'I was appointed staff officer to Wellington himself during my service in Spain, and watched far too many brave and resourceful officers of limited means lose out on the promotion they deserved.'

'I'm not your brother-in-law, sir.' The young man pointed out the flaw in Leighton's argument.

'No, not yet, but I assume you intend to offer for Marianne.'

'Of course, sir, but only if you were to set her free.' Stephen stared hopefully at the viscount.

'Damned if I see the need for all this waiting on my pleasure,' Leighton returned testily. 'Marianne and I have never been formally betrothed, and I can assure you I didn't give her a second's thought while I dallied with her sister.'

Clarissa gasped at his effrontery and rapped his arm with her reticule.

'And neither did she,' he added, with a complete lack of shame and some degree of truthfulness.

'Richard.' Clarissa could only blush and look outraged, mortified that her sister was staring at her open-mouthed with astonishment.

'I'll undertake to return this very afternoon and convey Marianne to her Aunt Constance, where she'll stay until the day of our betrothal,' he went on masterfully, ignoring the bloom on his beloved's face. 'We won't reach Bedfordshire until late tonight, but that's of no consequence to the matter in hand.' Leighton had taken control with a vengeance and Stephen could do no more than stammer.

'But—'

'Since most of society still believe Marianne and I are the ones to be betrothed,' Leighton ruthless dismissed Stephen's objections, 'it can hardly be thought improper for her to be seen in my company, especially if her maidservant is in attendance on her.'

'Sophie? Where is she?' Clarissa broke in.

'The last time I saw her, she was attempting to hide in the bushes on the edge of the park, my dear.' Leighton patted her hand reassuringly, another indication not lost on her sister.

'Before we leave, however, Stephen and I have an appointment with a magistrate. That official has, I hope, prepared a special licence for your marriage, but he must hand it over to you in person.' He bowed slightly towards the young couple. 'You have my felicitations.'

'But—'

'I took the liberty of informing the War Office of your upcoming nuptuals, and received their permission also.' He took an official-looking document out of one capacious pocket and passed it over to the young officer. 'I should report to your commanding officer as soon as you return to your regiment,' he advised. 'Tell him there were exceptional circumstances involved that made it impossible to seek his approval, as would be the norm.'

'But how can we hope to marry if I'm stuck out in Bedfordshire and Stephen remains here?' Marianne made her first attempt at mutiny.

'I'll contrive that much, never fear.' Leighton looked so certain they all believed him. 'Just as I'll contrive to marry Clarissa.'

'Couldn't I be the one to remain with Aunt Eleanor?' Marianne made a final plea to remain in London, closer to her future husband.

'No. I need Clarissa close by.' Leighton spoke with such an authority, they all felt bound to abide by it. 'Stephen will, of course, be welcome to stay at my house until such time as he has to return to his regiment.' He turned to Marianne. 'You too, once you've tied the knot. Now, if you're ready sir, we'll attend to our appointment at the magistrate's office.'

'I'm amazed you managed to arrange it so quickly,' Stephen blurted out.

'One of the few advantages of being at the head of a large and influential family,' returned Leighton dismissively.

'There's always someone on hand to help me obtain whatever I require.'

Once the men had left on their mission, Marianne turned to Clarissa, perplexed.

'I have you to thank,' she told her sister warmly, 'though how you did it, I can't tell.' She flung her arms around Clarissa and began to sob on her shoulder. 'I'm so happy, but what of you?'

'Why, it seems I'm to be married too.'

'To Lord Leighton.' Marianne couldn't keep the horror out of her voice, and nor could Clarissa keep her countenance straight.

'Of course,' she cried. 'Didn't he say he'd contrive.'

'Oh, Clarissa, you poor thing,' Marianne blurted out. 'I'll be free to spend my life with a man I truly love, but you? No, I can't let you waste your life by remaining silent. I once thought as you, that marriage to such a great man was all a woman could desire, but I was wrong. I've found true love at last, and so must you, however long the search.'

'I've found all I wish in Richard,' laughed Clarissa. 'He's truly the one I'll love for ever.'

'Well, he's not quite so top lofty as once I thought him. But love?' She stared at her sister nonplussed. 'Do you truly mean it?'

—◦◦◦—

CHAPTER TWENTY

A Scoundrel is Put to Flight

Thanks to their early start, and a swift conclusion to Stephen's business with the magistrates, it still lacked an hour to midday when Richard and Clarissa eventually emerged from the front door of the run-down hovel in which Stephen and Marianne had their apartment.

'Beware Dalwinton, guv'nor.' Teddy's less than genteel voice hissed out the words in a quiet undertone.

Leighton hesitated for no more than a moment while he took in the situation. Both Teddy and Tom were crouched awkwardly amongst the bushes that edged the property, and behind them, sitting cross-legged on the ground, was Marianne's maidservant, Sophie. Further off, across the muddy street, stood a small gang of toughs headed by Lord Dalwinton, evidently waiting to bar their exit. To Clarissa's dread it also included the young giant she knew only as Ben, Jem, apparently the owner of the building she'd burnt to the ground, an obviously bandaged Marston, Dalwinton's valet and a couple of nondescript characters holding makeshift, but no less deadly for that, cudgels.

'Do they know you're here?'

'I don't fancy so.' Teddy kept his voice at a whisper. 'Sophie spotted them first off, way over the far end of the park, and came to warn us. On my life, I didn't even know she was out there. Considering your situation I thought it best if we slipped across quick like, so I reckon they still believe they've got you trapped.'

'Stay where you are,' Leighton warned the groom, mouthing his words in a tone that was low and yet quite distinct. Then he turned to Clarissa, who'd been watching the welcome committee with a worried frown. 'You'd better make your way back to Marianne with Sophie; you'll be safer in the house.'

'No, Richard. This situation is as much my doing as yours. We'll confront them together.' Clarissa set her face, displaying a confidence she most certainly did not feel.

Leighton pursed his lips and looked as though he'd insist. Then just as suddenly he changed his mind. 'I haven't got time to argue,' he told her shortly. 'If we hesitate much longer they'll think we're frightened of them, or even suspect we're not alone. Come if you like, but stay behind me.'

He stepped forward, deliberately facing down their foes, who lounged truculently into the road to bar their way. Then, before Dalwinton had a chance to speak, took charge of the situation.

'Ben Fisher,' he began in a loud voice, seizing the initiative with both hands. 'I thought you were a fighter, not a fool to get mixed up in a business like this. If word gets out, as it undoubtedly will, your career's at an end. You don't need me to tell you that.'

He'd struck them at their weakest point as became obvious when the young giant began to hang his head and shuffle his feet like a naughty boy caught out by a particularly strict schoolteacher.

'Get off now and I'll think no more of it.' Leighton struck

again while the iron was hot. Ben was by far the most dangerous of their adversaries and it was important to nullify him.

'Stay where you are, Fisher.' Lord Dalwinton sounded like a strangled cat, caught on the hop by his declared enemy's tactics. 'He can't hurt you where he's going.'

'Get yourself back into fighting condition and find an honest manager to guide you,' Leighton continued to advise the young boxer. 'Your current one's a poor judge of character and he's more likely to see you in Hell, than fighting for the championship.'

'Go easy, Ben,' Jem chimed in, when his young protégé showed signs of retreating as Leighton had advised. Then he turned his wrath on the viscount. 'Your damned woman's burned my business into ashes,' he complained. 'Aye, and she's injured my good friend Marston too. I'll set the magistrates on the filthy bitch, you see if I don't.'

'It's my humble opinion,' chuckled Leighton, cheerily dismissing the improbable threat, 'that the circumstances surrounding the way the lady was being held in your attics in the first place may weigh unfairly with the magistrates' sense of justice. In brief, my lad, you're likely to find yourself experiencing life in Newgate Gaol, most probably, for the all too short period necessary to await your turn to dangle at the end of a rope.'

'You damned gentry, you're all alike,' Jem grumbled, with scant regard for the facts of the situation. 'The scales of justice never settles down on our side, and that's the truth.' He turned and stared at Ben, who'd taken advantage of his momentary loss of concentration to sidle away from the confrontation.

'Ben, lad,' he pleaded urgently, 'don't allow the gentleman to sweet talk you so. I'll see you fighting Cribb himself if you stays with me. That cove, he don't know what he's talking about, turning you against me. Ain't I always been honest with you, acting just like your own father ought?' He began to slink off in the wake of the young fighter, still arguing his case.

'Damn you, Leighton.' Lord Dalwinton recovered his poise at last and motioned the remaining toughs forward. 'Those two dolts leaving us doesn't change a thing. I've caught you at a disadvantage; you're hardly likely to win in a rough-house over such odds and then there's the safety of the lady at your side to consider. Admit the whole of your sordid deception and take the consequences, or I'll take her in lieu. There's no lack of places I can hold her fast, and I'll enjoy extracting the truth from her pretty lips.'

'It's a pity to disillusion you, my lord,' mocked Leighton and made a sign to his groom.

To the other's surprise, Teddy slipped out of the bushes levelling a pair of horse pistols on his noble target, nonetheless murderous-looking for all of their age. Tom stood at his shoulder, an ancient blunderbuss, almost as large as himself, held at the ready. Sophie appeared too, wielding a thick, knotted branch of oak in the manner of a weapon.

Dalwinton's underlings began to look decidedly nervous and even the loyal Marston edged back perceptibly.

'You're a pack of damned cowards, all of you.' Dalwinton tried to urge them forward, but they were having none of it.

'You didn't tell us we'd be up against the quality,' one of them complained. 'Nor guns neither.'

'I don't find no pleasure in mixing with swells.' Another took up the clarion call from a position at his companion's shoulder. And a moment later all of them were backing off fast, looking to follow the example set by their former comrades, who had disappeared into the park still arguing.

'Good of you to meet us in such a private place.' Leighton stepped forward to greet Lord Dalwinton, completely ignoring the valet, Marston, who was looking very uncomfortable since the tide of affairs had changed. 'Otherwise I should have instituted a search which may have resulted in a public exchange of views. So much more polite to discuss matters in private, don't you think?'

'Matters? What matters?'

'Your domicile,' replied Leighton easily. 'I don't think breathing English air will be healthy for you for a very long time ahead.'

'Are you threatening me?'

'Yes.' Leighton didn't think it necessary to wrap up his dirty laundry. 'If your conduct in this affair becomes known, no decent host or hostess will ever include you in their invitations and, if my word is to be believed, many of your less decent friends will cut you too.'

'Damn you, Leighton. I still don't know what you're planning to foist on the ton, but you can't tell me you want it nosed about. You're too proud of your family's good name to risk fouling it with any funny business.'

'Word is already out on the streets that Miss Meredew was attacked by a vicious gang and had to resort to a bold stratagem to escape her captors,' Leighton told him with a shrug. 'It wouldn't take more than a hint or two dropped here and there to implicate you in the plot.' He nodded towards the valet. 'I dare say some of the more perspicacious may already have noted the evidence provided by Marston's burns.'

'Impossible,' returned the malicious nobleman. 'You haven't had time to spread any such rumour.'

'On the contrary, I deliberately rose early and took the time to do so,' replied Leighton, elated that the shot had hit home. 'If

your involvement in such shenanigans became common knowledge …' His voice trailed off and he allowed the threat to ride
on the wind.

'I see no reason why I should flee the country,' blustered
Dalwinton, still convinced of Leighton's complicity in some
secret plan of his own. 'I can live without the sedate entertainments offered by your so-called decent hosts. As for the others,
my reputation is already less than stainless; I don't think my
role in abducting such an obvious charlatan will cause it to be
thought any more iniquitous.' He attempted a weak laugh as
though to gather his courage. 'Your own position is by far the
worse.'

'You will leave the country within the week,' insisted
Leighton, his voice hard as iron, 'unless you wish me to put an
end to your miserable life.' He'd stripped off his gloves while
they'd been talking and, taking them in one hand, he sliced
them hard across his opponent's face.

Dalwinton staggered back from the unexpected blow, his
countenance flushed scarlet by a rage he could barely hold
under control. For a moment the raw emotions played trans-
parently across his face and Clarissa, sheltering behind her
lover, felt certain he'd take advantage of Leighton's offer by
demanding immediate satisfaction.

'Damn you, sir,' he cried out, suddenly realizing what calling
out his remorseless opponent would mean. 'I won't fight you,
Leighton. I can't, not if you're determined to take our quarrel to
the death.' He laughed then, suddenly more confident of his
ground. 'No, you wouldn't dare kill me, else you'd have to flee
the country yourself.'

'I'd kill you in an instant,' Leighton ground out the ominous
threat. 'For insulting the lady I love, if nothing else.'

'I won't call you out then,' repeated Dalwinton steadfastly.

That he'd been frightened into believing the threats delivered by his relentless nemesis was evident to everyone present, and Leighton's whole attitude pressed home the point. 'You're a crack shot and so everyone knows. A master with the blade too.'

'Then I'll repeat the insult,' Leighton told him implacably. 'In public, somewhere you cannot refuse to seek satisfaction, unless you wish to shame yourself forever.' He laughed shortly. 'Your friends will force you into the quarrel, just as I've seen you do to others.'

The emotions continued to play over Dalwinton's face. He was a beaten man, as he eventually admitted. 'Come, Marston,' he commanded, and tried to retire in good order.

That much Leighton was not going to allow. He stepped forward and applied his boot to the other's posterior, sending him flying into the mud. Marston, loyal to the last, stood over his employer's prone form, ready to defend him, but instead took the brunt of the viscount's anger: a left to set him up, followed by a right that jolted him off his feet.

'If either of you should lay hands on my future wife again,' he told the cowering men with blazing eyes, 'I'm ready to risk the gallows to take my revenge.'

Dalwinton was scrabbling backwards in the dirt, his impeccable clothing already mired by the fall he'd taken. Marston showed less interest, his barely conscious body twitching at the feet of his noble opponent.

'Come.' Leighton offered his arm to Clarissa when Dalwinton scrambled to his feet and retreated with ignominious haste. 'I must return you to your aunt before I transport Marianne to Bedfordshire.'

CHAPTER TWENTY-ONE

Betrothals

Rather more than twenty-four hours passed before Clarissa saw Leighton again. She was engaged on a visit to Caroline in the afternoon of the following day when he finally appeared, tired and more than a little dusty, on her doorstep.

'Richard,' his sister greeted him with a distinct lack of filial respect. 'Where the devil have you been? In such a state, and your affianced bride here with me too. Whatever will she think?'

'Happily she is not such a numbskull as you, dear sister.' He advanced into the room and kissed her affectionately on the cheek. 'Now leave us alone, if you please, Caro. Clarissa, as you've hinted more than once since you discovered her deception, has not yet accepted my suit on her own behalf.'

'It would be most improper,' Caroline teased him, and made as if to sit again, only to be propelled by a strong pair of arms in the direction of the door. 'I'll order the champagne.' She made the offer her parting shot.

'No, I thank you, Sister.' Leighton was in no mood to be interrupted by a pack of servants delivering refreshment, however felicitous. His own tastes inclined towards a more intimate form of celebration, and he desired no audience to be a party to that form of revelry.

'My very own darling.' He approached Clarissa's seated form and suddenly dropped to one knee while he took her hands in his own. They felt cold from long hours of hard driving and Clarissa instinctively drew them close against her. 'I'm all too aware I've taken your endorsement of all my schemes for granted. I love you too much to give you up. Please, my darling, be mine. Marry me, I beg you.'

'Yes, Richard. Oh please, yes.' Clarissa's face blushed becomingly, but she no longer had any intention of pressing her sibling's claims ahead of her own. Not that it would be of the least use to do so, for neither her lover nor her sister seemed likely to heed her. Nor did she advance any objections on the impropriety of his spurning one sister in favour of the other. If it became necessary, she knew she'd follow him into exile from Town with no other remorse than a vague disappointment that she was the cause of him losing his own place in society. Not that it was likely to come to that! Richard would contrive to set all right again, just as he'd foretold. Just as he'd promised her.

For long moments, they stared deep into one another's eyes, before some devil within prompted her to tease him.

'Shouldn't you have approached Uncle John first?' she asked, with wide eyed innocence. 'I dare say he'd like to discuss settlements and prospects and such like with you, before the betrothal is settled.'

'Witch!' Richard quizzed her. 'How do you know I haven't?'

'Have you?' Clarissa stared at him in amazement. How had he found the time? Had he called on her uncle before his own sister?

'Of course I haven't. To speak to Markham would have been most improper when, as you very well know, he's not your guardian. I've settled the matter in proper form with your Aunt Constance, who has a great deal more consequence than you've shown thus far.'

'Then I'm surprised you shouldn't marry her instead.' Clarissa was playing with fire and she knew it, measuring the spark in his eyes with an air of mock innocence in her own.

'I don't marry her,' Richard answered tantalizingly, 'because she doesn't set a fire to my whole being.'

He rose all of a sudden and jerked Clarissa to her feet. She felt his breath warm against her hair, her own face cradled against his shoulder; suddenly, blood poundingly aware they were touching from breast to toe, her thighs and belly hard against his muscular form.

She expected him to embrace her then and there, and most probably kiss her into the stupidest daze, which, as she was well aware from previous encounters, he could do so easily. Instead, he surprised her once more, stooping lithely to sweep her off her feet and into his arms, before he adroitly spun around and settled back into the same seat she'd vacated only a few sweet seconds before.

Positioned on his lap and held fast against the hard, muscular wall of his chest she could only gasp in shock at his temerity. Indignation at being handled so cavalierly and the natural ardour of a woman in love fought a brief battle within her breast. Passion won and she eagerly turned her face up to be kissed, welcoming the fervour of his lips grinding passionately against her own.

His arms tightened around her, drawing her closer, and leaving her even more aware of the way her soft curves flattened against the strength of his masculinity. She felt a moment of panic and her palms pressed against his chest as though to push him away, but one slid, as though by accident, beneath the smooth superfine of his coat. Warm skin and rippling muscles seared her fingers through his thin linen shirt and she was lost. Her arms coiled lovingly around his shoulders, peeling back his coat, stroking the thick column of his neck and twining into the thicker hair at his nape.

She could feel the pleasurable sensation of his own hands greedily exploring her body, searching out her burgeoning curves, but no longer had the strength nor the will to protest. Her mouth lay open under his, his breath mixing inexorably with hers, while she returned his kisses with all the fervour of a more experienced lover. Her brain was intoxicated, unable to act of its own free will. She knew of that for certain, for her body was reacting to his sweet touch with a mind of its own, arching under the freedom of his loving, and ever bolder, caresses. One thigh, crushed helplessly against his virile masculinity, wilfully massaged his ardour, and encouraged him to new heights of passion. Desire had inflamed her virgin senses, igniting responses over which she no longer held control.

Clarissa could hear the knocking, but fuelled by the passion of the moment, thought nothing of it until Richard ceased his ministrations and looked around. Still reeling under the spell of her raw hunger for his enthusiastic caresses, she thrust herself fervently against him, seeking to draw him back into the vortex of their loving embrace.

Only then did she realize her position – their position. Caroline was standing in the doorway, eyeing their entwined forms with undisguised interest. Whatever would she think of them? Of her? The unbidden thought arose to the forefront of her mind; she was her mother again, helplessly tossed in a tide of desire over which she had no control. For the first time in her life she realized just how easily such a thing could happen.

'Caroline,' Richard gasped. He was equally as embarrassed

as his love at being caught in such a compromising situation, but much the quicker of the two to recover some composure. 'Don't you ever knock?' he complained, painfully aware of his own high colour and of the girl perched on his lap.

'Oh!' Clarissa was still unable to speak, appalled by her situation. Her face felt as though it was on fire and she was all too alive to the impropriety of her position, balanced precariously on a man's lap. Whatever had she been thinking of? Then she remembered of what she'd been thinking, and blushed all the more for her wanton behaviour.

Caroline, in the meantime, couldn't help but giggle at their embarrassment. Clarissa had staggered off her brother's lap and she almost fell into hysterics when he rose with stiff formality, stalking across the room with angry recriminations on his lips. Then he, too, was struck with the latent humour in the situation, and laughed out loud.

'I did knock,' Caroline assented. 'Several times, for I expected some celebration of the sort to be in progress. Then I peeped around the doorway' – she paused to curb the infectious giggles that looked likely to overcome her again – 'and discovered I had to knock again. Really, Richard. I thought you, at least, would be able to maintain some sense of decorum.'

She strode across the room to embrace her future sister-in-law, who still looked as though she'd like the floor to open up and swallow her whole. 'It was just such a scene when Sir Roger begged me for my hand,' she consoled Clarissa. 'I felt myself sunk quite beyond reproach at my enthusiastic return of his attentions. Though he,' – and she flung a fulminating look at her brother – 'at least, had the decency not to draw me on to his lap.' She blushed becomingly herself. 'Not on that particular day, at least.'

'Thank you, Caro.' Clarissa's thanks were heartfelt, and for all she felt the heat still glowing in her face, she was thankful to find her friend was attempting to put her at her ease rather than reproach her. Thank God it hadn't been another who had discovered them together. Such a passionate scene would make a pretty morsel for the gossips.

'Thank you? Thank you for nothing, Sister.' Richard had apparently regained his customary good humour, but his words made it obvious he still resented his sister's intrusion into their intimacy.

'As well I did interrupt you,' she replied, with a speaking glance, causing Richard to search his conscience. He should have held his passions in check, and well he knew it. He and Clarissa were not married as yet, and neither were they in their own marital home.

'I take it congratulations are in order,' Caroline went on to fill the ensuing silence, directing her speech this time towards her young friend.

'I can't think why you should want to congratulate me, or to welcome me as an addition to your family,' murmured Clarissa, still over-set by her frightening lack of restraint. 'Indeed, you shouldn't lay all the blame for what happened on Richard, either. My own emotions were wholly overthrown in a manner which quite puts me to shame.'

'So I should hope,' replied her hostess, laughing out loud with a complete lack of maidenly modesty. 'Richard would suffer a poor marriage otherwise.' She slipped a comforting arm around her friend's waist and led her to a chair. 'I hope you don't regret it.'

'Oh, no.' Clarissa blushed once again when she found herself admitting to the truth of the matter. It was true! If Richard should seize the chance to take her in his arms once more, then she would return his caresses with every fibre of her being.

Such a love could never be shameful, however embarrassing it was to be caught canoodling upon his knees.

'Then we'd better drink to your future happiness.' Caroline headed determinedly towards the bell rope, until Richard stopped her.

'No, Caro,' he told her. 'We have much to discuss before I leave again. All three of us.'

'Leave?' Clarissa asked the question in a quavering voice.

'I must, my darling.' He strode across the room, and for a moment Clarissa was worried he might draw her into his embrace again in front of his sister, and the next instant disappointed that he didn't. 'There are preparations to be made if our twin betrothals are to be announced to society.'

'Twin proposals?' Caroline had been listening with interest and demanded to know what he meant.

'I haven't time to explain,' Richard told her impatiently. 'Not now. Clarissa will bring you up to date once I've left.' He gave his love a speaking glance. 'In the meantime, Clarissa will need to refurbish her wardrobe.'

'I've already more than enough to wear,' she told him.

'All that you have belongs to Marianne,' he warned her. 'I intend to substitute her for you on the morning of the ball. You, yourself, will need to purchase a complete new wardrobe in utter secrecy, for you cannot be found in one of your sister's dresses. I dare say Caroline can help you there.' He turned to his sister. 'This must remain a secret between ourselves; Clarissa will have to deposit her purchases with you. Where can you hide them so no one suspects?'

'My dresser is to be trusted,' Caroline decided. 'She, at least, must know if we're to be successful in hiding such a wardrobe. I dare say Sir Roger might never suspect that my cupboards hold additional clothing, but I won't lie to him if he does.'

'Roger's fine, so long as he holds his tongue,' Richard agreed, but turned again to Clarissa with a warning. 'Your Aunt Eleanor must not be allowed so much as a suspicion. She might have her heart in the right place, but she's a complete goose when it comes to keeping a secret. I've little doubt she'd expose us all in a moment, quite without meaning to do so.

'Ready-made articles,' he continued, barely drawing breath, 'such as a lady might wear, are easily purchased. A shopkeeper might wonder at large amounts being sought so immediately, but I've never known the merchant yet who would balk at accepting money. Gowns and other such items are different. They take time to make up, and that's the one thing we haven't got.'

'I know of at least one fashionable seamstress who could undertake the task,' Caroline told him. 'There'd be a limit to the number of gowns that could be fitted in the time remaining before your ball, but enough to pass muster. Especially if she should also refurbish some of mine.' She studied Clarissa's figure carefully. 'We're much of a muchness so far as size is concerned.'

'Good,' Richard congratulated her. 'I'll also undertake to bring some of Clarissa's clothing from Bedfordshire when I return with Marianne.

'Clarissa,' he gave her one more task before he finished. 'You must be seen in Stephen's company as much as possible. He's residing in my house at present and it would be quite inadmissible for you to seek him there, but I'll engage to have him call on you at the Markhams' before the betrothals are announced. You may also look for him at other venues; Caroline can arrange such meetings. You will look all complaisance with him and allow people to think you a prettily behaved pair. It will otherwise look decidedly fishy when they marry in what might look like indecent haste.

'Caro, please give us a moment.'

Caroline stared at her brother, but did as she was bid, leaving the lovers alone again.

'We won't meet again until the ball to celebrate our betrothal,' he told Clarissa, tenderly taking her in his arms again and holding her close. 'I don't know how I'll hold myself in check,' he admitted, 'for I'm afraid our engagement will be of a longer duration than that of Stephen and Marianne. They have good reason to marry in haste, while we must endure the pleasures of others, whilst not taking pleasure in each other.'

'Dear heart,' she murmured and held up her lips to be kissed. 'We can always find an excuse to be alone.'

Richard, though shaken by a desire to ravage her until she could barely stand, kept the embrace to no more than a peck and stepped back with a hint of the barely restrained passion still lighting his eyes.

'Caroline,' he called out steadfastly, 'I'm ready to leave.'

CHAPTER TWENTY-TWO

Lover's Ball

On the morning of the ball, Richard made good his promise to return with Marianne, and to Clarissa's immeasurable relief, he'd transported Aunt Constance too. His carriage, boldly emblazoned with his arms, was tooled uncharacteristically in through the rear entrance of the Markhams' stableyard, where it broke its journey close by one of the house's several rear entrances. Clarissa was waiting there, having being appraised of its imminent arrival by the ever watchful Sophie, who'd returned to act as maidservant to the girl pending the return of her own mistress.

Clarissa raced across the cobbles and flung herself headlong into Richard's arms as soon as he alighted and continued to hold on to him while Sophie ushered her own mistress into the house. Providing she followed their plan to the letter, Marianne would then proceed along the deserted back corridors to a more appropriate position, ready to greet the official arrival of her aunt and sister. Thus the two sisters had no more time than to offer each other more than the briefest of greetings, though Marianne regarded the happy couple's affectionate embrace with startled eyes.

With Marianne safely smuggled into the house, Richard took the chance to steal a kiss before he handed his love into the coach and the ecstatic congratulations of her aunt, who'd evidently been brought up to date by the viscount on their various machinations.

Thus it was that Clarissa made her entrance through the front door on the heels of Aunt Constance, as Marianne made hers behind the Markhams, completely over-setting their peace, since they could hardly make out which girl was which, or even which one had last been in their custody.

That evening they all took their place in the line to welcome their guests, who having wondered at the likeness of the twins, wondered still more who Stephen was, and why he should take such a prominent place in the line up. In the event they were to be kept in the dark about his presence until Leighton made his speech later in the evening.

'I'd like to welcome you all,' he began, taking the place of Mr Markham, to that gentleman's secret relief.

John Markham had no wish to complain, but he still had no more than a hazy idea who Stephen was, or why he was on such terms of intimacy with at least one of his nieces. Marianne, wasn't it? Or perhaps Clarissa? Neither was he altogether sure which of his nieces Leighton meant to have. Surely he'd been betrothed to Marianne, albeit in secret, but then why had he caught him canoodling with Clarissa in the drawing-room? Or had it been Marianne after all? Damned if he could tell the two of them apart! He could only hope there wouldn't be a falling out between the two men when Leighton finally did decide. He didn't want to be party to a duel over the favours of the beautiful twins.

'No doubt you're wondering at the announcement of two

betrothals rather than the single announcement you might have expected,' Lord Leighton continued, quite undisturbed that, just like the Markhams themselves, none of the guests had wondered anything of the sort, since they had not been told of the twin betrothals.

'Captain Starkey,' – he indicated Stephen, standing straight and bright in his best regimentals – 'has the honour of winning Miss Meredew's hand – Miss Marianne Meredew.'

A hiss of conversation echoed around the Markhams' ballroom and Eleanor regarded her guests with some trepidation. She wouldn't put it past some of the gossips there to hold herself to blame over the incident when, for once, she was quite innocent of the deception. Indeed, she wasn't entirely sure she wouldn't blame herself also.

'I,' – and Richard tenderly took charge of Clarissa's hand – 'on the other hand, may be felicitated on my good fortune to win the other Miss Meredew's love. I'd like you all to meet Miss Clarissa Meredew, shortly to became my Lady Leighton.' He held up his hand to silence the growing murmurs from the assembled throng.

'As some of my closest friends could tell you, I had occasion to meet Clarissa some time ago.' He deliberately didn't reveal when or where he may have done so, and, since they had no memory of such an event, his friends could hardly have been blamed for feeling as vague about it as he himself. 'We fell in love immediately, but her guardian deplored the looseness of my lifestyle and thought an immediate betrothal inappropriate. Hence Constance' – he nodded towards the handsomely dressed woman at Eleanor's side – 'has only lately agreed to our becoming engaged.' He stuck to the truth that far, only telling it in such a way as to cover the deception that had been inflicted upon their friends.

'Marianne and I have been seen together on more occasions than I can count, but it was no more than a desire to seek a way in which Clarissa and I could be brought together that caused us to meet.' Not a direct lie perhaps, but certainly a mistruth, designed as it was to lead the gossips off the track. 'You will have seen,' he laughed, 'how quickly Marianne dropped me once her own beloved had recovered from his wounds.'

Since Clarissa had spent every free minute parading Stephen around the Town in the previous two days, this sally was received with the amusement it deserved. The lingering evidence of the young soldier's wounds was also apparent, and brought him much honour.

'Stephen and Marianne.' Leighton lifted his glass to toast them, swiftly followed by all society, encouraged in the ready acceptance of his story by his particular friends. 'They'll be married immediately,' he surprised them all again, 'since Stephen must return to his regiment post haste now that Bonaparte has slipped his leash on Elba and returned to rally his supporters in France.' He held up his glass again. 'Confusion to the French.'

The toast was drunk enthusiastically, for news of Napoleon Bonaparte's return to the country he'd led for so many years was a particular talking point. The spectre of war was haunting the country once again.

'Clarissa and I,' Leighton announced, 'will marry within the month. Indeed,' – and he smiled at her – 'I hardly dare wait that long.'